HER CYBORG RANGERS

SUSAN HAYES

SUSAN HAYES

Her Cyborg Rangers (Book 5 of the Drift: Haven Colony)

First Print & E-book Publication: January 2023

Editor: Amanda Brown

Published by: Black Scroll Publications Ltd.

DEDICATION

For my Mum and Dad, for all their love and support.

ABOUT THE BOOK

She dreamed of escaping Earth one day, but she never imagined the price she'd pay to be free.

Jade was a cyber-jockey. Emphasis on the word *was*. Now, she isn't sure who she is or what she wants to do with her new life.

No one else seems to know what to do with her either, including the two sexy cyborgs who are never far from her side but always just out of her reach.

Cyborgs. Batch-brothers. Survivors. They thought they were prepared for anything. Then they found her.

Wreckage and Ruin thought settling down would be simple, but living a quiet life has its own challenges.

The new ranger program might be just what they need, but it's not all they *want*. Drawn to Jade since the day they rescued her from mercenaries, they're trying to give her the time she needs to heal... and the space they need to keep their secret.

Three broken souls with the power to heal each other—if only they can let go of the past and trust in a future big enough for three.

PROLOGUE

Beyond the edge of civilized space is a newly colonized planet. It's a haven for the homeless, the hopeful, and those dreaming of freedom.

The beings who live here might be different species from vastly different worlds - but they all have one thing in common. Whoever they are, and wherever they came from, Haven is now their home.

The land is uncharted. The dangers are unknown. It's a world full of possibilities – for those willing to risk everything.

Welcome to Haven Colony.

1
___

THE BAR NONE was quiet for the moment, but Jade knew that wouldn't last. She'd thought the place was hopping in the winter months, but spring had brought even more customers flocking to the only human-run tavern in Haven colony. She had less than an hour to finish up with the bar droids and then test them to see if her upgrades had any unintended consequences before business picked up.

Kneeling behind the bar wasn't comfortable, but it was the only way to do a visual scan of the new code. While she worked, she did her best not to think about how much easier this would be if she still had her implants. They'd been ripped out of her during interrogation sessions she'd endured while a prisoner of corporate-backed mercenaries. She'd been one of the best cyber-jockeys in the known systems before the *fraxxing* mercs had caught her. Now? She was stuck in normal space forever, interacting with machines one keystroke at a time.

Of all the sacrifices she'd been willing to make to escape from Earth, she'd never imagined she would have to give up one of her defining qualities.

The calm was suddenly broken by the thud of booted feet on the tavern's veranda accompanied by rough male laughter. Someone shoved the door open hard enough it flew back to strike the wall with a loud bang.

Jade froze, her hands locking into fists as an icy chill flowed down her spine. She struggled to think, to move, to do *something* besides cower like a wounded animal, but she stayed where she was, teeth clenched, muscles screaming with tension, and heart pounding so fast she felt sick.

This was the other price she'd paid for freedom—panic attacks. Her time as a prisoner had left her with more than physical scars, and she was still learning how to deal with the sudden, gut-churning fits of panic that could be triggered by something as simple as a loud noise. She was broken in ways no nanotech or surgery could fix.

Her best friend Maggie hurried out to greet the customers, deliberately standing beside Jade and placing a steadying hand on her shoulder.

"Welcome to the Bar None. Take a seat wherever you like. I'll come around to take your drink orders in just a moment," Maggie said.

Several of the new arrivals rumbled words of thanks, some in Vardarian, others in Galactic Common. Thanks to the translators implanted in all of Haven's citizens, communication wasn't hampered by language barriers.

"You okay?" Maggie murmured once the others had moved off.

"As a duck in peach sauce," Jade replied. Her voice was tight and shaky, but she had breath enough to talk, so she'd call that a win.

Maggie snorted. "I swear you make up new expressions just to *fraxx* with me."

"Don't blame me. That was one of my father's expressions. I have no idea what it means either." The friendly banter was exactly what she needed to ground herself and regain control. She leaned against Maggie's leg, trying to slow her breathing and relax her knotted muscles.

It took a few minutes before she was calm again. Then she tapped the screen she'd been working on and activated the upgraded bar system with a still-shaking hand.

"The system and the droids are good to go. We'll want to test them before it gets busy," Jade announced as she rose to her feet, determined to keep it together in front of Maggie and the others.

"I'll test them. You're on a break," Maggie stated firmly.

Jade waved her off. "I'm fine. Just need to stretch

my back after being crouched on the floor so long. Remind me to talk to Anya about moving the central hub somewhere more accessible."

Maggie narrowed her eyes and then muttered low enough only Jade would hear her. "If you don't take a break, I will tell Anya *and* Saral that you're pushing yourself too hard."

"Whoa. You went straight to the nuclear option? How is that fair?" Jade protested. Saral and her two mates ran the tavern's kitchen, creating some of the best food Jade had ever tasted. The Vardarian female was also a natural caregiver, and she was determined to provide Jade with food, advice, and mothering whether she wanted it or not.

"Who said anything about playing fair?" Maggie smiled and nudged her shoulder against Jade's. "Grab a seat and relax for a few minutes. Saral has put together a plate for you already. If you don't stop for a meal soon, she's likely to come out here and glare at you until you've eaten every bite."

Jade managed a small but genuine smile. "She'd do that. Wouldn't she?"

"Without a doubt," Maggie agreed. "She cares about you, Jaybird. We all do."

Jade still didn't know how to deal with that. Until Haven, Maggie had been her only friend—the one person she trusted to have her back. Haven was different. The beings here were kind, accepting, and honestly concerned about her. It made her uncomfortable, especially because she couldn't offer much in return.

"I know, Magpie. It's just weird. You know?" she replied, using Maggie's nickname. Those names were part of their shared past, the years they'd spent on Earth, struggling to survive the hellhole that was the hive city known as Athens Two.

"I know. Remember, I've had a lot more time to get used to this place than you have."

"Long enough to fall in love with a hot as hell cyborg and learn to be a badass with that fighting stick of yours."

"*Kes'tarv*," Maggie corrected her with a snicker. "If Striker or any of the others hear you call it a fighting stick, you'll wound their egos."

"Yeah? Then I should probably say it to my bookend bodyguards the next time they start looming over me."

"They're not looming," Maggie protested and then threw up her hands defensively when Jade raised both brows and stared at her.

"Okay. They loom a little. They're protective of you. It's kind of sweet."

"No, it isn't. They get all growly with anyone who even tries to flirt with me, which doesn't happen much as it is. They've got cock blocking down to an art form, and I don't know why they're doing it. It's not like they're interested. They don't trust humans. Not that I can blame them." She shrugged. "A lot of us are assholes."

"Truth."

Maggie caught her by the hand and dragged her back into the kitchen. "Now, get some food and take a break. Shoo."

She did as she was told. Experience had taught her that a few minutes of rest after a panic attack lessened the aftereffects significantly. Saral waited in the kitchen. The Vardarian female made a disapproving clucking noise and then handed her a plate stacked high with the Vardarian version of sandwiches with a side order of spicey fried tubers.

"Sit. Eat. Rest," Saral instructed. "You should have mates to take care of you, but yours are slower to come to their senses than most."

"Mine?" Jade shook her head. "Who would want me?"

Saral snorted. "Is this some sort of human affliction? That none of you can see what is as clear as the sky on a sunny day to everyone else?"

"I have no idea what you're talking about. Now, I'm going to follow your advice and find somewhere out of the way to eat this delicious meal. Thank you." She nodded to Saral and then to her mates, Antas and N'tev, before fleeing. Saral was kind, generous, and determined to see everyone around her as happily mated as she was. Jade appreciated the female's good intentions, but she was too broken for any man to want, no matter what their species.

The closest she had to male company were Wreckage and Ruin, but they treated her like a little sister, not a romantic interest. If she couldn't even interest the two battle-scarred cyborgs who shadowed her like a pair of overprotective gargoyles, what chance did she have with anyone else?

She slipped into the tiny space they called a staff break room and sat down to eat. Three mouthfuls later, the door opened again.

"No need to check up on me, Saral. See? I'm sitting and eating as instructed."

"It's not Saral, but she did tell me to make sure you were eating." Phaedra's distinct voice and unexpected laughter filled the air, and Jade leaped to her feet. "Phreak? Uh, I mean Princess Phaedra. What are you doing here?"

The fuchsia-haired woman smiled and settled her very pregnant body onto the nearest chair. "I'm here to recruit you."

Wreckage swung the axe with practiced ease, each strike taking another bite out of the trunk of the tree he and Ruin had chosen to harvest from the area around their cabin. The spring sunshine felt good on his bare back, the warmth soaking into his scarred skin. Every stroke of his blade filled the clearing with a crisp, satisfying *thwack*.

Birds sang in the trees and the breeze stirred a hundred branches and a thousand leaves as it blew through the forest. On the far side of their cabin, Ruin prepared a freshly fallen tree, trimming off the branches and peeling the bark. They'd need more logs to have enough to expand their home, but they had months of good weather ahead and plenty of incentive to get the job done.

It had only taken a single winter for them to realize they'd need more space if they were going to get through the cold, dark days of winter without killing each other, though it got easier once their young charge had been granted full citizenship and returned to live in the colony. Cam had proven himself trustworthy and loyal to his new home.

If they moved back into Haven, they'd also be entitled to separate residences that would both be bigger than their hand-built domicile, but neither of them were ready for that. The colony was nice, but it lacked the calm and peace of the forest. After a lifetime of war and then confinement on Reamus Station, Wreckage needed solitude and quiet. The only exception to that rule was the company of his batch-brother, Ruin. The other colonists generally understood and gave them space, welcoming them when they came into town and leaving them alone the rest of the time. It was what they wanted. At least, it had been. Wreckage wasn't sure about that anymore.

Another swing of his axe made the tree shudder and groan as it gave way. "Timber!" Wreckage called out as he moved adroitly out of the danger zone.

The tree dropped to the ground in a cacophony of breaking branches and tearing wood that ended with a thump he felt through the soles of his boots.

"Why do you insist on saying that when you have no idea what the *fraxx* it means?" Ruin demanded, his voice clear despite the distance between them.

"Because it's faster than yelling, 'Hey, asshole, pay attention to the big tree about to crush you!'" Wreckage called to his batch-brother.

Three seconds later, a fist-sized rock soared over the roof of the cabin. "Hey, asshole, watch out for the rock about to smack you!" Ruin yelled and then added, "Huh, your way is faster. Point to you."

Wreckage didn't bother to move. The rock would miss him by ten meters or so. *"That gives me ten points. You know what that means?"* This time he sent the message via an internal comm link so he didn't have to shout.

"Fraxx," Ruin swore inside his head. *"Already?"*

"Yep. Which once again confirms that I'm the smart one. We're going into town tonight and the first round is on you."

Ruin didn't respond, which wasn't normal. The

two of them bickered like it was a sporting event, and they were both vying for the championship.

A moment later, Ruin appeared around the side of the cabin. His shoulders were tight, his hands fisted at his sides, and his face was twisted into a scowl. *Great.* Ruin was in one of his moods.

"Problem?" he asked, even though he already knew the answer.

Ruin ran a hand through his dark hair and grunted before answering. "We've been in town too much lately. We should stay away for a while."

"Because everyone is going to forget what we look like if we're gone long enough? The Vardarians might, but the cyborgs have perfect recall," Wreckage reminded his friend. This argument had been going on as long as they'd been on Liberty, and he was tired of it. Eventually, someone would figure out their secret. At some point, they'd have to face the consequences.

Ruin's lips twitched into a momentary snarl. "I know. And I know we've had this conversation so many times we can both recite the other's point of view verbatim, but I..." he trailed off and smacked his fist into his open palm.

"You think I'm looking forward to having that conversation?" Wreckage shot back.

"You're acting like it."

"Seriously? That's the best argument you've got?" Wreckage set down the axe and folded his arms across his chest. "We can't hide out here forever."

"It's only been a year," Ruin argued. "What's the harm in giving things more time?"

"More time for what? For our brethren to figure it out for themselves? Or for someone to put the moves on Jade while we're out here hiding?"

"We're not hiding." Ruin smacked his fist into his palm again, but it lacked the force of his previous action. "We're keeping a low profile, but we see Jade every week, and we're there when she needs us. She's still recovering. It's too soon."

"There's a small *vething* gap between too soon and too late," Wreckage grumbled. That thought had been niggling at the back of his mind for a while now. Jade was brave and tough for a human, but she was still *human*. They were so weak they'd created cyborgs to fight their wars for them. Jade was stronger and braver than most, but she'd endured hardships and cruelty for most of her life. Then she'd been captured and tortured by mercenaries. He and Ruin knew too well what kind of scars that left.

Jade needed time to heal. But how much? If they left her alone too long, someone else would move in and take the woman they wanted for themselves.

That couldn't happen. She was the only woman he and Ruin had ever wanted for more than a night. He'd felt it since the moment he'd carried her out of the mercenaries' ship. She belonged with them, but only when she was ready. Until then, he wanted to stay close enough to ensure they didn't miss their moment.

"Is Jade the only reason you want to go into town so much these days?" Ruin asked.

"Not the only reason, no. Your cooking is almost as bad as mine, which means the only way to get a decent meal is to pay someone else to make it." Their future plans included having enough off-grid energy to support a food dispenser, but that wouldn't happen for at least another year, especially now they were dividing their time between the cabin and their new duties as rangers. Between training sessions and the time they spent patrolling and mapping the areas around the colony, there just weren't enough hours in the day. Not that he was complaining. Staying active made it easier to forget about the past, and sometimes he managed to push himself so close to exhaustion he actually slept for a few hours before the nightmares woke him.

Ruin nodded in grudging agreement. "Whatever that was we had for dinner last night made me nostalgic for the days of nutri-bars and algae paste."

Wreckage winced. "You cooked it. Don't you remember what it was before you turned it into a burnt offering?"

"Something I found in the back of the cooling unit. It was only slightly green and fuzzy, so I figured it was safe to eat."

"You bastard. I don't know whether to laugh or worry you poisoned me." Even if Ruin was telling the truth, it wasn't really anything he had to worry about.

His medi-bots granted him accelerated healing and protection from illness... or food poisoning.

Ruin's grin faded after a few seconds, and his expression turned thoughtful. "Do you think Jade would like to come out here? You know, for dinner?" He held up a hand. "We'd do takeout, of course. But the place is looking good these days. I'd like to show her around and see what she thinks."

"Of what? Of the woods? The cabin? Or us?"

"All of it. This is our home. It could be hers, too. I mean, she doesn't have a permanent job yet, and she hasn't been assigned housing. We could offer her another choice."

Wreckage didn't know whether to laugh or smack his batch-brother upside the head. "Whoa. We haven't even asked Jade out on a date yet and now you're suggesting we ask her to move in with us?" He shook his head slowly as he imagined all the ways that could go wrong. "Do I need to contact Skye and some of the other cyborg women to explain to you what a terrible idea that is?"

Ruin cringed. "*Fraxx*, no. Do not involve the women. I'll never hear the end of it."

"*We* would never hear the end of it, because they'd blame me for letting you even consider the idea. As clueless as I am about dating, I do know we're going to need to make more of an effort than that. We'll need to romance her and make her feel special."

"She *is* special." Ruin's sun-bronzed features collapsed into another scowl.

"Yeah, she is." Wreckage took a deep breath before locking eyes with Ruin. "So, what are you saying? Do you think it's time we let her know?"

"Not yet." Ruin chuckled ruefully. "As you just pointed out, we're clueless about this dating stuff. I think it might be time to start making plans, though."

Wreckage clapped his batch-brother on the shoulder. "I think you're right. We can start tonight while we're having dinner at the tavern."

"I still don't think it's smart to go into town so much." Ruin ran a hand over his close-cropped beard. "I could grow this out and you could, too. That worked before."

"It worked because you and I were kept in isolation most of the time. I don't intend to spend the rest of my life that way. If we do that, we're not really free."

"I know," Ruin said and then followed it with a heavy sigh. "But when they figure it out..."

"Then we'll deal with it."

"My way is easier. Feed her dinner. Show her around. Offer to move her in and take care of her. She might say yes," Ruin grumbled.

"And she might laugh in our faces," Wreckage retorted. "That's not a chance I'm willing to take. We've still got time. We'll work on a plan and then dazzle her with romance and flowers and stuff. Maybe Striker has some suggestions. He managed to get

Maggie to fall for him and he's a sullen, silent bastard most of the time."

Ruin grunted in agreement. "That he is. If he can figure out romance, so can we. Besides, we're much better looking."

"Truth. We'll clean up the worksite and then shower and head into town. I need a brew and decent food. If we're in luck, Jade will join us."

Ruin nodded. "I'll admit, she's worth going into town for. That, and I'm tired of looking at your face."

"And I'm tired of eating charred food that may or may not have been green and fuzzy," Wreckage shot back.

Once he was alone again, he set to work cleaning up the site and storing the tools for tomorrow. He smiled and hummed to himself as he worked, already looking forward to tonight. They weren't ready to make their move, but they were ready to make a plan. By the time Jade was ready, they would be, too.

2

JADE RECLAIMED her seat and pushed the plate full of fried tubers toward Phaedra. "Help yourself. Saral's portions are all Torski-sized. Then could you please explain what you meant by recruiting me?"

Phaedra uttered a pleased little laugh and took several slices. "Thank you. I'm starving. No one told me that eating for two meant I'd be hungry *all* the time. All I seem to do these days is eat, pee, and take naps."

Jade grinned. "Better you than me. How much longer?"

"No one's certain, but best guess is another two months or so. By then I'll be so big I won't fit behind my desk." Phaedra munched on a chip before continuing. "Oh wow, these are good. I think I've found my new craving. I'll have to tell the guys to order some to take home with us."

"Your mates are here, too?" The prince wasn't a common visitor to the Bar None.

Phaedra devoured another chip before speaking again. "They're here and they are driving me nuts. I can't go anywhere without one or both of them tagging along these days."

With a sigh, Phaedra sat back in her chair and placed a hand on her stomach. "And that brings me back to the reason I'm here."

Jade ignored the flutter in her stomach and waited for Phaedra to explain. This offer—whatever it was—seemed to be more important than just a job.

"How much do you know about the cyber-security system we have here on Liberty?"

"I know you and a small team of Vardarians run it. I assume there aren't any cyborgs on your team because none of them were designed for this kind of work and haven't expressed an interest in learning."

Phaedra nodded. "We tried to recruit some cyborgs, but after so many years as captives, none of them are interested in a desk job that probably feels too much like being locked up again. I don't blame them."

Jade laughed. "That's just what it looks like from the outside. Being in cyberspace is the best kind of freedom in the galaxy." Her laughter died away, stolen by a pang of loss and regret. "I miss it."

"I can only imagine." Phaedra gave her a sympathetic smile. As the only other cyber-jockey in the colony, Phaedra understood better than anyone what Jade had lost. "Forgive me for asking, but what about the surgery Dr. Li suggested while she was here?"

"It's still a possibility, but none of the Vardarian healers are familiar enough with human physiology or cyber-implants to do it. Even Li admitted there'd be some serious risks. Like, I could fry the few implants I still have or even die the first time I jack in." She tapped the port behind her ear. "This isn't the life I want, but it beats being dead."

"I hear that. But being jacked in isn't the only way to access the datasphere." Phaedra wiggled her fingers in front of her. "You could go old school."

"You mean sit behind a screen and type out commands?" She shuddered in dramatic horror. She'd just spent an hour doing that to get the bar system updated, and it had been teeth-grindingly tedious. Doing that as a full-time job? No.

"Not *that* old school. I'm talking about a holographic interface. It's not the same. I know." Phaedra lowered her voice. "But we need you. *I* need you. A storm's coming, and we're not ready for it. You are a damned good cyber-jockey, and that's a rare skill set around here. The Vardarian diaspora attracted more artisans and business types than techies, and their culture doesn't have anything like human cyberpunks."

"What's coming for us this time?" For a new colony, Haven had plenty of enemies. Torex Mining had been strong-armed into releasing their claim on this planet so the Vardarians could set up a colony here. It had cost the corporation unimaginable sums of lost profits, and they were still trying to steal what resources they could without being caught. Then there were the Gray Men, a shadowy cabal that had once wielded great power but were now scattered and weakened, though still dangerous.

"The usual suspects, and maybe some new ones. We're calling one group the Shadows. We think they're an offshoot of the Grays, but they seem to have a different focus."

Jade recalled the recent plague that had swept through the Vardarian population thanks to a nano-swarm smuggled onto the planet and used to disable the aliens' nanotech.

"Keeping humanity pure and untainted?" she asked, thinking about the reasons one of the first human colonists had given for releasing the swarm.

Phaedra wrapped her arm protectively across her swollen belly. "That's the story they're telling, but that's never the whole truth."

She'd seen this sort of thing play out more than once in the hive city she'd managed to escape. "They want power at any cost, and they're willing to set the galaxy on fire to get what they want."

"Exactly. We're a target because Haven is offering women like you a chance to escape Earth, which means the corporations will lose one of their largest pools of recruits. We're everything the Grays, or the Shadows, want to eliminate—a place where different races coexist in peace and cyborgs are free citizens instead of possessions." Phaedra straightened, her shoulders square and her jaw set. "We're a ray of hope in the darkness and chaos they want to create."

"And you want *me* to help protect the colony? I'm only a citizen here because you convinced the council that Maggie and I got here legitimately, despite the fact I hacked in and boosted our odds."

"I didn't convince anyone. I told the truth." Phaedra stated. "Believe it, Jade. You belong here."

"I'm not sure I do." The confession was out of her mouth before she could stop it.

"I am. Remember, I wasn't born a princess. I'm a cyber-jock, just like you. We're survivors who did some questionable things to some questionable people, but that's not all we are."

Her next words left her mouth tasting of ashes and regret. "I'm not a cyber-jockey anymore. I'm just... broken. Your skills are legend, Phreak. You don't need me."

"That's where you're wrong." Phaedra's expression turned stormy. "There's something else I need to tell you. In a few days, I'm going to make an announcement that's going to make some waves and attract more problems. When that happens, I'll have to step back. Hell, if my *mahoyen* have their way, I'll be locked away in a secret, secure bunker somewhere until this baby is born... or longer."

"What? Why?"

"*Scrava?*" Phaedra asked.

"*Kush*," Jade replied, confirming she understood. It was a hacker code language, used for conveying messages when security wasn't assured. She hadn't used it in a few years, but she could still manage the basics.

"My *mahoyen* and I have chosen not to alter our child's genetics. They won't be pure Vardarian, but a hybrid. Not everyone will accept that. Not even here. When the empress hears..." Phaedra shook her head.

"The heir is going to be half human? You're not going to make waves. You're going to trigger a *fraxxing* tsunami."

"Tell me about it. And that's not all. Apparently, a group of Vardarians believe their species needs to return to the old ways. They're called the *Liq'za*. Their influence is one of the reasons my mates came looking for a new home, and they are a potential threat to what we're building here."

Jade threw up her hands in disgust. "For the love of gravity, I swear every race in the galaxy has the same flaws, even if we don't have a single chromosome in common. Why is that?"

"Your guess is as good as mine." Phaedra relaxed and even laughed a little. "But now you can see why I need you. No one else can do what we can, and I'm going to be a big, pregnant target soon."

"And if they find you online..." Jade had lost

friends to online attacks. It was too difficult and expensive to do often, but it did happen. She wouldn't let that happen to Phaedra. Haven was a good place, and even if it wasn't the home she'd hoped for, it was all she had.

"I'll do it," she told Phaedra. "When and where?"

Phaedra dropped back into Galactic Standard. "Is tomorrow too soon? That would give me some time to get you up to speed before the news breaks. The where is up to you. Half of the team works out of an office on the grounds of the palace, including me. The other half are on the plat." She pointed upward.

Working in the palace meant she'd cross paths with Yardan, the permanently grumpy and suspicious spymaster. He'd made it clear during her many debriefings that he didn't trust her, and the idea of working in the same place as he did wasn't appealing.

The orbital platform position was tempting. She'd miss the freedom of roaming under an open sky, but the Hub offered her a chance for a new start, away from everyone whose concern for her was a physical weight that threatened to smother her if she didn't get out from under it.

She had reasons to stay and reasons to go. She'd need time to decide.

"I can start tomorrow. Anya is really only keeping me on so I have something productive to do. I'm not sure where I want to work, though. Can I give you my answer tomorrow? You know, after I've seen the setup down here, talked to my friends, and thought it all through?"

"Tomorrow is fine." Phaedra reached across the small table to squeeze her hand. "You have no idea how happy I am that you agreed to this. My backup plans involved getting Maggie involved and then escalating from there."

"Escalating?"

"I have no shame. It was Maggie first followed by enlisting the help of River, Anya, and then Saral."

"You are the second person to threaten me with Saral today. Does she know how much everyone fears getting on the wrong side of her?"

"Oh, she knows." Phaedra grinned and then struggled to her feet. "I better get out there before my mates break down the door and carry me home to bed."

"More naps?" Jade asked.

"Sure. Naps. Let's go with that." Phaedra snickered and waggled her brows. "I hope when your day comes, you're smart and fall for just one guy. Keeping up with two is going to be the death of me."

Two guys. In her dreams, that's what she wanted, but she knew it wasn't going to happen. Wreck and Ruin thought of her like a little sister, nothing more.

That was another reason to move off-planet. She wouldn't be around when Ruin and Wreckage fell in love with someone else. She wanted them to be happy, but that didn't mean she needed to witness it firsthand.

As much as he bitched about making the trip into town, Ruin never complained about the actual journey. Not since they'd invested in a pair of hover-bikes. They weren't the safest mode of transport, but thanks to their cybernetically enhanced reflexes, he and Wreckage handled them with ease. They were fast, agile, and gave him a taste of what it would be like to fly the way the Vardarians could—only faster.

The forest beneath him flashed by in a blur and the wind roared in his ears as he opened the bike's throttle up and increased his lead on Wreckage.

"It's not a race," Wreckage spoke through their internal channel.

"You're just saying that because you know I'm going to win."

A second later Wreckage poured on the speed, attempting to catch up. *"Never going to happen."* He sent to his batch-brother and then sped up yet again. He'd been secretly tuning up his hover-bike for weeks in preparation for this moment. Wreckage didn't have a change of beating him to Haven.

The bike flew like a meteor across the sky, and he gave a whoop of unbridled joy. *This* was freedom, and as much as he struggled with so many elements of his new life, he was thankful for the chance to experience what it meant to be free.

His enjoyment was cut short by an internal

message from their friend, Striker. *"Wreck. Ruin. We need to talk."*

Words to strike fear into anyone, even a cyborg like him. *Fraxx.* What fresh hell had their enemies thrown at them this time?

"We're here," Wreckage answered before he could.

"And ready to throw down to protect the colony," Ruin added.

"It's not the colony you need to worry about. This is..." Striker paused, and his next words were accompanied by a sense of embarrassment so strong it bled through the connection. *"It's about Jade."*

"Is she hurt? What happened?" Wreckage demanded. Ruin figured his batch-brother had missed the subtle emotional tell in Striker's statement and had gone straight to the worst-case scenario. Typical. Wreckage didn't care about much in this galaxy, but he'd die to protect the things he did. One of those things was Jade.

"She is unhurt. What happened is that Phaedra offered her a job on her cyber-security team."

Unease gripped his guts, twisting the loops into tight knots. *"That's not the part we need to worry about. Is it?"* he asked.

"She's got a choice of locations. One of them is on the Hub."

It took Ruin a moment to remember that was the new, official name of the main orbital platform circling Liberty. *Re'veth.* If she went to the Hub, they wouldn't be able to keep an eye on her, protect her... *be with her.*

"Is now the moment to say I fraxxing told you so?" Wreckage sent via their private link.

Ruin reached back with one arm and flipped an obscene gesture in Wreckage's direction while he continued to talk to Striker. *"How do you know about this?"*

"Maggie," was all Striker said. Of course. Jade and Maggie were best friends. It made sense Jade would talk to her about it, and Maggie must have told Striker because... He swore aloud in every language he knew. Maggie and Striker had to know about their interest in Jade. When did his fellow cyborgs start paying so much attention to other people's business?

"Did your lovely and oh so attentive mate have any advice on how we should proceed?" Wreckage asked.

Striker laughed. *"She suggests you two idiots get your asses into town and talk to Jade about your feelings."*

"Feelings?" Ruin winced. *"We're cyborgs. You know we don't do that."*

"If you want Jade in your lives, you'll have to change that. Trust me. It's worth the pain," Striker said, still laughing. *"Oh, and she says if you do show up, come to the kitchen door of the tavern. She'll let you know where to find Jade."*

"We were already headed that way. We'll see her soon," Wreckage sent and Striker signed off.

Ruin slowed his hover-bike to a crawl and waited for Wreckage to catch up.

The moment he did, Ruin turned to him with his hand raised. "Yes. You were right. Yes, this counts as another ten points all by itself. Don't be smug."

Wreckage barely cracked a smile. "We'll talk about that later. We have a bigger problem."

"Jade," they both spoke her name at once.

"I thought you said she'd need more time." Ruin glared at his batch-brother as if this was all his fault. He knew it wasn't, but he said it anyway.

"Like I'm an expert on anything to do with humans in general or women of any species," Wreckage scoffed. "I thought she'd need longer. Seems I was wrong."

"No kidding."

"How many do you think know about this?" Wreckage asked.

"At least two that we know of. The number is probably higher." He sighed. "Knowing our friends, there's probably a betting pool going already."

"*Fraxx.*" Wreckage scrubbed a hand over his hair. "You ready for this?"

"To talk about my feelings? *Veth*, no. But what choice do we have? The way I see it, this is a now or never moment."

Wreckage finally smiled. "You're in?"

As far as he could tell, they were out of time and options. Just like any other battle, that left them with two choices. Retreat or attack. He'd never retreated in his life. "I'm in. She's worth it."

"Yeah, she is. Guess we better go tell her. And then take her out for dinner somewhere besides the Bar None." Wreckage pointed at Ruin. "And no, that doesn't mean we're taking her back to the cabin."

"And subject her to your cooking? We're trying to impress her, Wreck, not traumatize her."

They locked gazes for a moment, both of them aware that after this, nothing would be the same again.

"Let's do this," Wreckage said and accelerated toward the colony. Ruin fell in beside him as they flew toward Haven... and Jade.

They parked the hover-bikes on the shore and walked the rest of the way to the tavern. The Bar None stood in the middle of a broad bridge that linked the two sides of the colony. Vendors lined both sides of the structure, some in simple tents or carts while others now had proper storefronts. Beings of all sizes, species, and ages wandered through the stalls, exchanging greetings as they shopped.

The tavern doors were open, spilling light and the sounds of merriment into the evening air. They passed the main doors and went around to the kitchen door. It was closed, so Ruin raised his hand and knocked loudly enough he'd be heard over the bustle and chaos of the kitchen.

The door opened, but instead of Maggie, he found himself face to face with Saral.

"Hello. We're here to talk to Maggie."

"And Jade," Wreckage chimed in.

Saral gave them a bemused look. "Maggie is busy at the bar and asked me to talk to you if you showed up." She opened the door wider and gestured them inside with a hand holding a dangerously sharp knife. "Took you long enough."

Ruin didn't know what to make of her comment. They'd been on their way before hearing from Striker. "Hover-bikes only fly so fast."

Saral snorted in derisive amusement. "That's not what I meant, but never mind. Jade volunteered to help set up the stage for tonight's entertainment. Straight through that door." She pointed with the knife in a way that made Ruin's instincts twitch.

"Thanks, Saral." Wreckage shoved Ruin in the back, pushing him inside and past the knife-wielding female.

The air was warm and thick with the rich scents of savory meals and sweet desserts. Saral's mates glanced up from their work as they entered, both of them grinning.

"Finally made up your minds?" Antas asked.

"Better get in there before she decides to leave," N'tev said, his grin widening.

Saral closed the door and laughed. "Go in and good luck. Better late than never."

"Thanks. I think." Wreckage nodded to the cooks,

and then the two of them made for the door to the tavern. "*Apparently they know, too,*" he sent.

"Apparently," Ruin replied dryly. Not bothering to use their private channel. They'd deal with that issue later. Right now, he had only one thing on his mind—convincing Jade not to leave Haven.

3

———

THE BAR WAS so loud she could barely hear her own voice as she tested the sound equipment for tonight's performance, but midway through her check the entire tavern lapsed into silence, leaving her simple, "Test. Test. One. Two. Three," echoing in the empty air.

Jade looked up to see what was going on and found herself face-to-chest with two very familiar figures. She didn't need to see their faces to know it was Ruin and Wreckage. She'd memorized everything about them. The broad expanse of their chests, the way their shirts clung to their shoulders and slid over hard, sculpted muscle.

"Hey, guys. I didn't know you were coming into town tonight." If she had, she would have put more effort into her appearance while pretending she wasn't.

"It was a last-minute decision," Ruin said.

She raised her gaze to their faces just as Wreckage shot his batch-brother a dirty look.

"What he meant to say was we wanted to see you. So, uh, here we are." Wreckage spread his big hands in front of him and smiled.

Fraxx, did she love his smile. When he smiled, she saw the man beneath the scars and brooding blue eyes. His skin was a dark golden color from his time outdoors, and his dark brown hair had shocks of pure white that marked scars she'd always wondered about. Jade caught herself before she stared too long and smiled back. "You should have let me know. I'm just finishing up here and then I planned to take a walk. I've got a lot on my mind today."

"Yeah." Ruin reached up to rub the back of his neck. "We, uh, we heard about that."

"You did?" She didn't bother to ask who had leaked the news. Phaedra wouldn't have said anything, so it had to be Maggie.

"Magpie!" she leaned around Ruin to glare at her friend working behind the bar.

Maggie gave her a look of almost saintly innocence. "What? Was that supposed to be a secret?"

"You know it was!"

"Oops."

Everyone in the tavern was watching their exchange with interest, and Maggie's last comment made many of the patrons laugh.

"Don't blame Maggie. She was doing us a favor,"

Wreckage said before she could say anything more to her former best friend.

Jade blinked at him, suddenly at a loss for words. "Huh?" was the best she could manage.

"Before you make up your mind, we wanted to talk to you," Ruin said and then looked at Wreckage.

"Yeah. But not here. Can we go somewhere else?" Wreckage raised his voice and turned to glare around the tavern. "Preferably a place where everyone present isn't part of a betting pool."

Raucous laughter and whistles filled the bar. What the hell was going on?

Wreckage bent down until his mouth was near her ear. "Just say yes."

"Yes." The word was out of her mouth before she could think about what she was doing.

Without warning Wreckage lifted her off her feet and swung her into his arms. She uttered an undignified squeak of surprise, her fingers catching the collar of his shirt and holding on for dear life. He carried her toward the door, and when she looked over Wreckage's shoulder, Ruin was only a step behind, his blue eyes so dark and stormy they looked almost black. Was he mad at her? At Wreckage?

From a corner of the room came a familiar voice. "Alright. Mark the time and let me know if you think you won," Thrash said.

"I am going to kill that *bakaffa*," Wreckage growled under his breath.

"I don't understand. What are they betting on?" Jade had no idea what was going on, and she wasn't enjoying it. Well, being snuggled up to Wreckage wasn't bad, but she could do without the rest.

"Us. They were betting on us." Ruin's words rumbled like summer thunder, and his handsome features were twisted into a scowl that made him look even more dangerous than normal.

"Us?" Her confusion was giving way to frustration.

"We'll explain once we're alone and away from here. Otherwise, Ruin or I might decide to come back and break Anya's rules about fighting in her bar."

"Uh, hello? You can't just pick me up and carry me off. That's called kidnapping."

"You said yes," Wreckage reminded her.

They were outside the bar now and headed for the quieter side of the river that used to belong to the cyborgs.

"I'm revoking my yes and changing it to an *oh hell no*." She smacked her hand against Wreckage's cast iron chest and tried her best to glower. "Put me down."

"I'd rather not. I haven't had a chance to hold you like this since the first day we met."

Well, that wasn't what she'd expected him to say. Still, she needed to make her point clear. Maggie had warned her about the cyborgs and their need to be in charge. "I can't carry on a conversation with both of you this way. And I get the feeling this is a three-person conversation."

"It is," Ruin said. "And she's right, Wreck. You need to put her down."

To her amusement, Wreckage pouted for a second before finally sighing in resignation. "Okay. But for the record, I'm happy to pick you up again any time you want, Jade."

"Right. Good to know." Her confusion returned, and this time it brought its friends, uncertainty and what the *fraxx*.

Once she was back on her feet, she turned to look at the two cyborgs who had watched over her from the moment she'd come to Haven. They'd guarded her as she recovered from her injuries, visited the Bar None just to sit and watch her work, and escorted her to every social event in the colony. They were her protectors, and she hoped they were her friends, but they'd never shown the slightest interest in her as a woman until now.

They stood side by side now, and she crossed her arms and tipped her head back so she could look them both in the face. "Explain."

"About the betting or what we wanted to talk to you about?" Ruin asked.

"The second one. We'll circle back to the first thing once I know why you're here tonight. Maggie obviously told you about my job offer, but that doesn't explain why you need to talk to me. This is my decision to make."

"It is." Wreckage took her by one hand as Ruin

took her by the other, the two of them moving so that all three of them were now walking to the shore hand in hand with her in the middle.

Wreckage gestured to the shore up ahead. "Our hover-bikes are parked on this side of the bridge. That's the only reason we're going this way. We thought maybe you'd like to have dinner with us. Eat while we talked."

"This is a date?" her bewilderment must have shown on her face because both men stopped and looked down at her with expressions so muddled she couldn't read them at first. Surprise, concern, and... holy hell, was Ruin *blushing*? He was the one she thought of as the darker of the two brothers—both in looks and temperament. His hair was black and long enough it was always falling into his eyes. His beard was black, clipped short, and shaped with sharp, crisp edges. She'd often wondered if he used a straight razor to get them so perfect.

Why couldn't she stay focused when she was around the two of them?

"It could be a date. If that's what you want," Ruin said.

This could not be happening. Six months of hoping, and they chose *now* to ask her out? Only, they didn't ask. They'd picked her up and carried her out while everyone laughed and cheered... and talked about winning a bet. Son of a starbeast!

"That bet was about us, as in you two asking me out?"

Wreckage looked sheepish and both of them were so adorably vulnerable she wanted to hug them. Or smack them. "You knew about this and didn't tell me?"

"What? No!" Ruin shook his head. "We had no idea until today. We thought no one else knew we were interested." He glanced back over his shoulder toward the tavern and growled.

"Well, I can tell you that at least one person didn't know about it. Me! Why didn't you say anything? And for that matter, what are you interested in exactly? Because I'm so confused right now I can't tell."

"We *fraxxed* this up," Wreckage said softly.

"Royally," Ruin agreed. "But Wreck is going to explain now."

Wreckage swung his gaze over to Ruin. "I am?"

"Yup. Because as much as it pains me to admit it, you're better at this stuff than I am. You talk. I do. And doing is not going to help right now."

Jade couldn't help herself. She laughed. "I'm sorry. I'm not laughing at you. I just..." she burst into another peal of laughter and clung to their hands in case they tried to pull away. She didn't want that. Whatever this was, she didn't want them to leave, and if this was what she hoped, she wouldn't leave them, either.

Both men stayed quiet until she regained control.

"Are you okay?" Ruin asked, looking more than a little worried.

"I'm better than okay. I think I know what this is about."

"And that made you laugh?" Wreckage looked crestfallen.

"No. That was me venting nervous energy while enjoying watching the two of you bicker. Now, tell me why you're here. Please?"

"We came to see you because we don't want you to leave Haven. We've been waiting, trying to give you space while you recovered," Wreckage said.

"Because humans are delicate, and you needed time and space to heal," Ruin added.

"Delicate?" Jade nearly choked on the word. "You think I'm *delicate*?"

She'd been called many things in her life, most of them insulting, but no one had ever described her that way. She was a survivor and a sometimes thief. A former cyber-jockey with black market implants that had been torn out of her flesh, leaving her with scars not even nanotech could fix.

Ruin glared at his batch-brother. "You said that was why we were waiting."

"And you wanted to invite her out to the cabin for our first date and then suggest she just move in then and there," Wreckage retorted.

"Whoa. You want me to move in with you?"

Both men nodded and then stopped almost at the same moment. "Eventually," Wreckage said.

"If you want to," Ruin added.

"I think you two missed a few steps in this process. Haven't either of you dated before? I mean, I know you were created during the Resource Wars so obviously things were busy and difficult, but didn't you ever have girlfriends?"

"No." Ruin shrugged. "You're the first woman we…"

"Wanted," Wreckage finished.

She listened to them, fascinated by the way they finished each other's thoughts. They were clones, she knew that. But they'd survived so much together they behaved almost like they were the same person at times. Yet at other times, they were nothing alike.

"You want me?" She needed to hear them say it again. This was what she'd dreamed of. What she'd hoped for.

"Yes." Wreckage turned to face her, drawing her around by her hand until they were face to face.

Ruin released her hand and moved in behind her, his big body pressed to her back and his head bowed over hers. "We always have. But you needed time."

She basked in the warmth of their bodies as they held her between them, cocooned in their masculine strength. "Time? Yes. Six months of it? No. What I really wanted was more time with you."

"Is that another yes?" Wreckage asked, his voice deepening to a low, husky tone she'd never heard from him.

This was it. The moment she'd been waiting for. "It is. Yes. But it comes with conditions."

Both men stiffened slightly, something that was easy to notice given they were pressed up against her. "What conditions?" Ruin asked.

"Well, for one thing, I'm not moving in with you tonight," she said with a soft chuckle. "I want to get to know you. *Both* of you. That's my second condition. I don't want to date one or the other of you. I don't think that would work."

"We both want you," Ruin said, dropping his mouth to her ear. His breath fanned her skin and sent a frisson of desire dancing down her spine.

"Good. That's... good." It was getting hard to think straight when they were so close to her.

"What else do you want from us?" Wreckage asked.

The question was layered in so many meanings she didn't dare think about it too much or she'd be tempted to do something rash. After all, she'd waited this long. What was a few more days?

"I want to be courted." It was an old-fashioned word, but she couldn't think of a better way to describe it. She'd had boyfriends before, but there wasn't time or energy for romantic gestures when everyone had to hustle just to eat. Those relationships were more about escaping reality and avoiding the empty ache of loneliness than anything else. She wanted more than that.

"Courted," Ruin repeated. "By us?"

"Courted by the two of you. As in flowers. Dates. Holding hands and stuff like that. You know, the things that make your heart beat faster and makes you feel like you're walking on air." Granted, she was basing some of this on vids and romance novels, but there had to be *some* factual basis to those stories. Right at this moment, she was in lust with Ruin and Wreckage, and if she gave in to that feeling, she was afraid she'd miss out on something better. Something *real*.

"I've never experienced that," Ruin confessed.

"Me either. Clearly we've been missing out." Wreckage grinned at his batch-brother and then looked down at her. "As you might have noticed, we're not good at this kind of thing. You might need to help us out."

She laughed. "I'd love to. How else will you know what I've been dreaming of?"

The moment she spoke, both men went silent.

"You've dreamed about this?" Wreckage asked in a voice gone deep with desire.

"I want details," Ruin whispered in her ear. "I want to know all your dreams, little bird."

Jade's knees went shaky and her head spun faster than the thoughts chasing around her mind. Holy nova, this was happening. She'd been so wrong about them, and they'd been wrong about her. Delicate? Pfft. She was a scarred, broken mess, but they knew that already.

"I'll tell you when I'm ready." She twisted around

so she could see both of them looming over her. "But only if this is really what you want. Be sure because if we do this, I'm playing for keeps."

They spoke together. "We're sure."

She let out a soft breath and mustered a smile. "Okay then. Step one, we need to go out on a date."

"Tell us where you'd like to eat and we'll take you there," Wreckage said.

She cocked her head to one side and then shook it slowly. "Not tonight. What about tomorrow instead?" That would give them all time to think. This might be what she'd been hoping for, but the suddenness of it felt odd. Did they really want her, or was this all because they'd learned she might be leaving?

Neither looked happy about the delay, but they both agreed.

"Then we'll go out tomorrow night. A real date, just the three of us." Hope and happiness bloomed in her chest like small stars.

"You won't move to the Hub?" Ruin asked.

"You two just gave me a damned good reason to stay here. I'll tell Phaedra I'd like to work with her team at the palace." She considered telling them that the only reason she'd have moved was so she didn't have to be around when they found someone special, but she decided to keep that to herself for now. If things didn't work out, she could always ask Phaedra for a transfer later.

"Good," Wreckage murmured. Then he lowered

his head and claimed her mouth with his. It wasn't a gentle, tentative kiss. His lips slanted over hers with barely restrained hunger, hot and demanding.

A tiny moan escaped her lips to buzz against his mouth and he made a low sound of need that sent ribbons of desire unfurling through her veins.

When Wreckage raised his head, his blue eyes blazed with a heat that made her want to fall back into his arms for another kiss, but she resisted temptation... for now at least.

"We haven't even been on our date yet," she said, trying to ignore how breathless she sounded.

"That one was on credit," he said.

"If he gets one on credit, so do I." Ruin hadn't finished speaking before he had her turned to face him.

He placed two callused fingers beneath her chin and tipped her head up a second before he kissed her. Where Wreckage's kiss had been hungry, Ruin's kiss was pure possession, raw and demanding. His lips moved over hers and the hand that had been beneath her chin slid past her ear to tangle in her hair.

She swayed toward him while Wreckage moved in closer behind her, sandwiching her between their hard bodies. Both of them were focused on her, Ruin's mouth on hers, both her hands still entwined with theirs. It was intense, and intimate, better than anything she dared to imagine.

When the kiss ended, she was left with a giddy feeling and knees that threatened to buckle if she tried to walk. And that was after one kiss each. What would it be like if—or when—they took this to another level?

Honestly, she couldn't wait to find out.

"We'll walk you back now," Wreckage said.

"Slowly." Ruin brushed a kiss to the top of her head before moving away. "Unless you'd like me to carry you?"

"Tonight, we can walk." She positioned herself between them, still holding their hands. "Tomorrow? I guess we'll have to see."

4

———

Between last night's romantic revelations and the jitters that came with starting a new job, Jade had a restless and relatively sleepless night.

Fortunately, the medi-bots she'd gained after her arrival at Haven kept her fatigue at bay by boosting her metabolism. In fact, the nanotech in her bloodstream increased her reflexes, endurance, and even her strength.

Between the medi-bots and the abundance of food here, she was fitter and healthier than she'd ever been on Earth. She was curvier too and loved dressing to accentuate her new look, though she always wore long sleeves to hide the scars on her arms. She didn't like to look at them, and she couldn't imagine anyone else did, either. Well, no one but Wreckage and Ruin. They'd been there when the wounds were fresh, and they'd stayed with her while she healed. They'd already seen her at her worst, which was why she thought they weren't interested in her romantically.

She chortled into her mug of liquid motivation. That was what she called the blend of coffee and ja'kreesh she enjoyed every morning. Ja'kreesh was the Torski version of coffee, potent enough to keep a two-legged tank on the go for a day or more. It only took a spoonful to amp up her coffee, and she enjoyed the way the two flavors blended into something rich with just a hint of spice.

Breakfast was simple by local standards, but to Jade it was a decadent feast. She toasted slices of bread baked the day before and then slathered the thick slices with jam made from several kinds of local fruits and berries. She had an entire shelf dedicated to different jams and jellies she'd bought at the local market. Nothing like them existed in the hive city where she'd been born. Fresh fruits and vegetables were a rare luxury. To feed so many people, the main crops were fungi and algae, supplemented with vat-grown proteins and nutri-gruel. Just the thought of the tasteless gray glop she'd eaten for years made her shudder with revulsion.

Her thoughts flitted from subject to subject, and it took her longer than it should have to realize it was because she was nervous. She wasn't sure whether the new job or tonight's promised date with Wreckage and Ruin had her more anxious. Both events were important to her, and neither of them were sure things.

No risk, no reward, she reminded herself.

She paced around her temporary home as she drank her coffee and devoured the thick slices of freshly made toast. The apartment she lived in was above the Bar None and had originally belonged to Anya. Well, technically she still owned it, but the tavern's owner lived with her mates now and had offered it to Jade for as long as she needed.

The apartment was cozy and welcoming, and it was certainly convenient for popping into the tavern downstairs, but it wasn't home. She liked it well enough, and the meals Saral insisted on cooking for her were wonderful, but Jade never felt like she *belonged* here. Her thoughts went down yet another rabbit hole as she considered her life. Maybe she didn't feel at home here because she hadn't had a real home in years. Her parents had both died in an outbreak of some unnamed fever that had torn through the lower levels of the city. After that, her eldest brother, Marco, had signed a lifetime contract with one of the shipbuilding corporations. He'd left with promises that he'd come back and get her and their brother as soon as he could.

They'd never heard from him again.

By the time she was fifteen, her only remaining brother died of a pharma overdose, but she'd been fending for herself long before Tino's death. He gave up on life and her not long after Marco left. She wasn't like her brothers. She was a survivor who would never abandon the ones she cared about.

Never.

Jade crossed over to the window and looked out onto the street below. Across from her were the shops and vendors that filled the bridgeway, stretching out in each direction until they reached the shores of the Sterling River and the colony that spread out beyond. Entire neighborhoods had been built and left empty for future colonists, all of them free for the taking.

Eventually she'd leave this apartment so someone else could enjoy the space. Maybe once she settled into her new job she would move into one of the empty houses on offer... A little voice whispered from the back of her mind. *Or maybe I'll move in with Wreckage and Ruin.*

She immediately derailed that line of thought. Don't jinx it, she told herself. Don't even think about it. It's too soon. For all she knew they could have already changed their minds. The thought made her stomach queasy. *Please don't let them change their minds.*

She hadn't had many dreams come true in her life. If this fell apart before it even began...

A quick check of the time told her she still had a half hour before she was due to arrive for work, but she couldn't stay here anymore. It was time for her to go. She stopped just long enough to run a comb through her hair one more time, smoothing out the dark waves and trying to muster a confident smile despite the butterflies fluttering in her stomach. With one more deep breath, she turned and headed to work, only to stop the moment she opened the door. A bouquet of spring wildflowers was resting on the mat outside the door to her home. They looked fresh and no dew had collected on the petals, so they couldn't have been here long. Blooms of red, pink, yellow, and even orange exploded in a riot of colors bound with a bit of blue ribbon.

At least, she thought it was ribbon, but once she picked it up, she realized it wasn't cloth at all but several lengths of wire braided together. That made her smile and even laugh a little. She knew who had left these for her without even reading the note she could see among the blossoms. Who else would use wire to bind the flowers they must have picked themselves? It had to be Wreckage and Ruin.

She pulled the note out of the bouquet and read it. It was written in a bold blocky hand and stated.

Have a good first day at work.
We can't wait to see you tonight.
W & R

She read it three times in a row before grinning foolishly. Thankfully no one was around to see her moment of weakness. She brought the flowers inside, set them in a mug of water, and then slipped the note carefully into her pocket.

Her day was already off to a wonderful start.

The palace guards were expecting her and escorted her across the grounds to the doors of the palace. Phaedra greeted her with a cheerful smile and an unexpected hug.

"I'll confess I wasn't sure you'd come. I know I'm asking a lot after all you've been through, and I'm grateful you're here." Her smile faded for a brief moment and Jade saw the deep concern in the princess's eyes. "We need your help."

"I need to do this. Not just because I want to help, though that's a big part of it. I..." Jade shrugged and ran a hand over the loose sleeves that hid the scars on her arms. "This is important to me, too."

"I know," Phaedra squeezed her arm and then led her inside. "Come on, let me give you the tour. Then I'll introduce you to the rest of the team and you can flex your cyber-jockey muscles. I suspect the others are going to be impressed by your skills."

"Let's hold off on talking about my skills until you've seen me in action," Jade said. "You might not be all that impressed. It's been six months since I even attempted to enter the datasphere."

Phaedra laughed. "You might be rusty, but I know what you're capable of." She lowered her voice. "We've known about each other for a long time, Slyce. I know what you did to try and make things a little better for your city. Don't sell yourself short."

Jade hadn't heard that name since before she'd left Earth. Slyce was her alter ego, the hacker who rerouted supply deliveries, especially meds and food, to those who needed it. She'd run scams, twisted corporate security codes into knots, and stolen scrip from anyone she thought could spare it. Phaedra had once been Phreak, and she'd been a legend to cyberpunks like Jade.

Now, that legend had asked for her help, not just for herself but for Haven. If ever she was going to have a home, this was it.

"I'm here, and I'll do my best." She let her gaze drop to Phaedra's rounded belly. "For you and for your baby."

"Thank you."

Their conversation continued as Phaedra showed her around. The place was an eclectic mix of residential areas, workspaces, and even a small but elegantly appointed throne room.

The halls bustled with activity, the air humming with an almost melodic blend of hushed conversations, hurried footsteps, and an air of importance that was like nothing she'd ever experienced.

The palace was also quite beautiful, with high ceilings, polished tile floors, and a sense of age that belied the fact this palace hadn't existed until recently.

"The room we work in is just down here," Phaedra said and gestured ahead of them.

Deep, booming laughter came from an open doorway. The voice sounded familiar, but Jade couldn't place it, so she risked a glance into the office as they passed by.

It was Yardan, the dour and distrustful spymaster, laughing with his head thrown back and a wide grin on his face.

Jade nearly tripped over her own feet in shock and turned to give Phaedra a quizzical look. "Yardan laughs now?" she whispered.

Phaedra grinned and nodded. "Oh yes. Amazing, isn't it? Falling in love has done wonders for that male."

"I'm glad. I wondered how Skye could be happy with anyone that... grumpy."

Phaedra snorted. "I'd like to point out that you have a date with Wreck and Ruin tonight. If there was a grumpy competition, those two would be in contention for a spot on the podium."

"And they'd probably bicker about which of them deserved the gold." They were both laughing when they reached the door to her new workspace.

"Come on in and meet your teammates. I'll arrange for a holographic meet and greet with the staff on the platform later today."

Her coworkers were two unmated Vardarian males named Allax and Lorn. They were *anrik*, a blood-bonded pair who would claim a female together. Jade noticed them both inhale deeply when she entered the room. It was something she'd gotten used to since joining the colony. Each time she met a new Vardarian male, he tested her scent to see if she was his destined mate. In her heart, she knew she wasn't destined to be claimed by one of the winged aliens. Her new teammates were friendly, polite, and handsome enough to attract the eye of any single female in the colony, but she wasn't single anymore.

At least, she hoped she wasn't.

Their workspace was a cyber-jockey's wildest dreams come true. It was secured against all sorts of electronic surveillance and hacking using both human and Vardarian tech.

There were computer systems more advanced than she'd ever seen with faster-than-light transmission speeds and a variety of ways to interact and manipulate data. She noted more bells and whistles than she could inventory and a few gadgets she was certain were illegal everywhere in the known galaxy.

"This is..." Jade turned to beam at Phaedra. "Holy *fraxx*. This is lux! How did you get a hold of all of this gear?"

Phaedra smirked and tapped her chest. "Being a princess has its perks. Come over here. This is your workspace."

Still dazed by everything she'd seen, Jade's sense of amazement went into overdrive as she sat down in front of her station. The chair was so comfortable it was like sitting on a cloud, which made sense once she realized it wasn't attached to the floor. Instead, it hovered and moved with her, almost as if she were...

She swallowed back tears and looked over at Phaedra. "I'll barely be able to tell I'm not jacked in."

"That was the idea."

Moving through cyberspace was the closest a human could come to flying. Jade had missed that sensation every day since her implants had been torn away. This wouldn't be quite the same, but it would be close enough.

She strapped herself into the chair, testing the restraints before slipping on the cranial interface band and donning the interactive gloves. Then she activated the holographic display. Instead of a single surface, a shimmering dome rose up around her, surrounding her with the familiar world of the datasphere. Jade whooped with joy, shook out her hands, and reached out for the data flowing past her. "Let's do this."

5

WRECKAGE HADN'T BEEN this nervous since... He ran through his onboard database and realized he'd never experienced this sensation before. It wasn't the breath-holding anticipation of combat or the reflexive moment of fear-fueled aggression that came every time his cell door had opened. This was something new.

They'd spent most of last night and a good portion of today brainstorming ideas and doing research on what exactly Jade wanted from them. The answers had been less than clear. Some options were easy to eliminate. The colony had taverns and even a few nightclubs, but that wouldn't be much different from eating at the Bar None. A theater was under construction, but that didn't help with their planning. They didn't even know if Jade liked that sort of thing. How the hell were they supposed to plan a date for someone they wanted to know better when they didn't know Jade well enough to be sure what she liked?

Eventually, they'd agreed that was probably the point. As much time as they'd spent with Jade, they still didn't know a lot about her. Tonight, they'd start changing that.

They approached the stairs that led up to Jade's apartment atop the Bar None, neither of them speaking.

"Who knew going to war was easier than dating?" Ruin muttered.

"And you thought we could just take her to our place and ask her to stay." Wreckage wasn't letting go of that anytime soon.

"Yeah, well. If you try to tell me you thought it would be this hard, I'll call you a *fraxxing* liar."

"I had no idea. I'm starting to think the Vardarians have it easy. If she smells good, she's your mate. Go have hot sex for a few days and figure it all out later."

Ruin grunted in agreement, but before either of them could say anything more, they heard footsteps on the deck above them. They lapsed into silence and looked up as Jade stepped into view.

"Re'veth. *Did we know she was this hot?*" Ruin sent via their internal link.

Wreckage didn't answer. All he did was stare.

They'd dressed up for the occasion, but Jade had transformed herself.

Loose black slacks flowed over her legs, with slits in

the side that showed off the leather boots that clung to her calves. She wore a Vardarian style top with an ornately stitched, rounded collar. The dark fabric split just below the line of her breasts, exposing the golden skin of her stomach. Her arms were covered in a gauzy fabric that gathered around her wrists, the dark fabric the same shade of deep brown as the curls that tumbled around her face and fell to her shoulders.

She held a shawl of soft, woven wool in one hand.

Neither of them said anything, but she smiled as if they had. Then she swirled the shawl around her shoulders and descended the stairs toward them.

"Thank you."

"For what?" Wreckage asked. Most of his attention was on Jade and his mouth was operating on auto pilot.

"For looking at me like that." She joined them on the ground, her eyes aglow with happiness.

Ruin took her hand and raised it to his lips. "I'm looking at a goddess right now. There's only one way to do that. With reverence."

Wreckage didn't know whether to be impressed at his batch-brother's smooth line or pissed the bastard had upped the ante already. Then he spotted an opportunity and made his move.

"Reverence and adoration," he said, moving in to sweep her hair out from under her shawl. The silken strands caressed his skin, and it was all he could do not to use it to tug her in for a kiss.

Patience. He reminded himself.

"Oh, wow." Jade's cheeks darkened, and she lowered her gaze. "Where have you been hiding this version of yourselves?"

Ruin released her hand and then winked at her. "We can learn new things... when properly motivated."

Wreckage took note of her elevated body temperature and increased heart rate. She liked being the center of their attention. How had they missed this until now?

"Would our goddess like to accompany us to dinner?" Ruin asked before Wreckage could.

"Your goddess would like nothing better." Jade took each of them by the hand as they fell in on either side of her. "Where are we going?"

"Earthly Delights," Wreckage told her as they walked. "It's new."

Jade laughed. "You're telling me there's a restaurant called Earthly Delights out here, in a colony with almost no humans in it?"

"Yep. Better yet, it's run by two Vardarians and their cyborg *mahaya*."

"And this is one of the many reasons I love Haven. Anything can happen here." She looked up at him, her eyes bright with emotion. "Even things I never thought possible."

"This is more than possible," he said.

"It was inevitable," Ruin finished and shot him a smug look over Jade's head.

"This is not a competition," Wreckage sent.

"*Sure it is. And if we do this right,* everybody *wins.*"

"You guys realize I know you're talking to each other right now. Right?" Jade spoke up.

"We were just discussing how lucky we are, and how beautiful you look," Wreckage said.

"*Nice save,*" Ruin said.

Jade's lips twitched into a brief smirk. "Sure you were. I know you better than that. You were probably insulting each other."

"No comment," Ruin said. "But that is the point of tonight's date. We want to get to know you better."

"And let you get to know us."

"I'd like that." Jade went quiet for a moment and then looked back up at him. "Will you tell me how you got the scars on your head? Was it something they did to you at Reamus? Or before?"

Well, that was direct. They hadn't even asked her about her first day at the new job yet. But that was one of the things he liked about Jade. She wasn't one for small talk or inane conversation. She said what was on her mind, just like them.

"Before. You know Ruin and I fought in the Resource Wars?"

"I did. Maggie told me. She wanted to be sure that the two of you were safe for me to be around, so she asked Striker."

"She thought we weren't safe?" Ruin almost growled the last word. "As I remember it, we rescued her *and* you. What else did she want?"

Jade laughed and leaned in to bump Ruin with her shoulder. "She was protecting me. After all, I got shot protecting her during that rescue."

Her tone was light, but he heard the pain hidden beneath the humor. He remembered the moment he'd first set eyes on her. He'd followed Striker into the mercenary's grounded ship, intent on getting Maggie back.

In the ensuing fight, he'd watched Jade, already bloodied and battered, throw herself into the line of fire to protect her friend. The blaster bolt caught her in the thigh, but she'd kept joking through the pain. He'd fallen a little bit in love with the fierce little human right then and there.

"Next time there's danger, promise you'll leave the fighting to us," Ruin said.

"Why? Because I'm a *delicate* human?"

Wreckage winced. She hadn't forgiven them for that choice of words yet. "No," he said. "Because we were designed to be killers. It's encoded into every cell of our bodies."

"We didn't choose our names. They were given to us by the techs before they cleared us for active duty." Ruin jabbed a thumb at his chest and then at Wreckage. "They're not so much names as job descriptions."

Jade wrinkled her nose. "Maybe that was true back then, but it's not true anymore."

"We haven't changed," Ruin argued.

She huffed. "I think you have. You talk about being killers, but since you came to Haven, the only ones you attacked were the ones attacking your home. You've both signed up to be rangers, and I'm pretty sure their mandate is to protect Haven and the planet rather than, you know, commit random murder. You're not killers. You're protectors." She squeezed his hand. "Just like you've been protecting me since I got here. Though I'm still not sure what you were protecting me from."

"Anyone and anything who wanted to hurt you," Wreckage said.

"And other males," Ruin said.

She turned to look up at Ruin. "Other males? So all those times the two of you were impersonating glowering gargoyles was to keep other guys away?"

"Gargoyles?" Wreckage asked, more than a little insulted.

Ruin had apparently run out of smooth lines and had reverted to his usual bluntness. "Yes."

"You were running other males off, yet neither of you thought to say anything to me about it?" She glanced up at Wreckage. "And yes, gargoyles. Big, mythological creatures of stone that stand sentry, guard things, and don't talk."

"We're talking now." He guided her through the streets of Haven, deftly dodging other pedestrians while keeping an eye on the skies overhead. Despite what Jade had said about them changing, some things were the same. He would always stay alert for threats. Haven was a good place to live, but it wasn't without its dangers.

"We are talking," Jade agreed. "And I still want to hear how you got those scars."

Jade was having one of the best days of her life, second only to the day she'd been reunited with Maggie and discovered her best friend had fallen in love in the time they'd been apart.

Now... She glanced up at the two handsome men accompanying her tonight and allowed herself a tiny moment to hope. Maybe it was her turn.

"He got those scars saving my ass," Ruin said.

"It was my fault. I'm the one who hit the tripwire," Wreckage replied.

"Tripwire?"

Wreckage explained, his big hands moving as he talked. "We were tasked with taking out the enemy's forward operating base. It wasn't big, but they'd had time to burrow in and set up more defenses than we'd expected."

"Yeah, because the intel we got was dangerously incorrect. We'd have been better off going in blind," Ruin said.

"She asked me to tell the story, not you. You have your own," Wreckage said to his batch-brother before continuing. "It was late in the night cycle. It had been raining for weeks, and the whole area was just a big mudhole. The main portion of our forces were actively engaging the enemy while we broke through and made for their base."

She sensed tension in his body and realized he was reliving events as he told her the story. Damn it. She'd have to be careful not to ask too many questions about their time as soldiers. She hadn't realized it still affected them so much.

"Then Wreck lived up to his name and wrecked the plan by tripping a bounding mine," Ruin chimed in.

"What is that?" she asked.

"A kind of explosive that jumps up into the air a meter or so before detonating. That way, the force of the explosion strikes the midsection instead of just a soldier's feet and legs," Wreckage explained. "The thing is, it takes a second for the mine to ascend before it goes off. If you're fast enough, you can drop to the ground and get out of the blast zone."

"But you didn't do that."

"No, he didn't. He called out a warning to the rest of us and then turned and used his own body to protect us from the worst of the blast." Ruin gave his brother a fond look. "*Fraxxing* idiot should have died."

"But I didn't." Wreckage's jaw tightened, and she saw a flicker of something dark cross over his features, like storm clouds blotting out the sun.

"I'm glad you didn't, or we wouldn't be together tonight." Jade stopped walking and twisted around to face Wreckage. "Remember the day we met?"

Wreckage nodded. "I'll never forget it."

"You were tending to my injuries, and I said something about being a broken mess." She smiled up at him. "What did you tell me as you picked me up and carried me out of there?" The memory of what he'd said had been a bright moment in one of her blackest days.

To her delight, the shadows left Wreckage's eyes as he spoke the same words he'd said to her that day. "We're all broken, sweetling. It's what we do with the pieces that matters."

The three of them lapsed into silence for several seconds. Then Ruin cleared his throat and said, "*Fraxx* waiting. If you don't kiss her right now, I will."

"Wait your turn, asshole." Wreckage growled at his batch-brother, but his eyes never left hers.

"Thank you," Wreckage whispered before releasing her hand to pull her into his arms and kiss her.

Hard muscles against her body, a hot mouth slanting over hers, his fingers tangling in her hair. She let go of Ruin to focus on Wreckage, one hand on his shoulder and the other stroking over the streaks of white in his hair. He shuddered as she caressed him, a low groan falling from his lips to buzz against her mouth.

Time ceased to exist. They could have stood in the middle of the sidewalk kissing for a few seconds or a few hours. She had no way to know. All she was certain of was that she didn't want him to stop... though eventually he did.

She heard herself make a soft sound of protest, but before she could do anything more, Wreckage stepped away and Ruin took his place. He framed her face in his hands, drawing her head up until she was looking at him. Blue eyes, a strong jaw, and a nose that had been broken and healed crooked.

"Hello, little goddess. Did you forget about me?"

Jade shook her head slightly. "Never."

"Good." His kiss was scorching, but his touch remained gentle, the callused tips of his fingers tracing the line of her jaw. She rose on her toes to kiss him back, her hands finding his shoulders and clinging to them to keep her balance as the world spun around her.

From somewhere nearby, she heard laughter. "About time!" a male voice called.

"Go away, Storm," Wreckage snarled at the speaker.

"I'm going! I'm going! Have fun!"

"Sorry about that," Ruin murmured before releasing her.

"Don't be. I don't care who sees us." Veth. Had she just said that out loud? This was not a conversation topic for their first date.

Both men turned to stare at her. "You don't?" Wreckage asked.

"Tell us more," Ruin said.

Her cheeks went hot, and she shook her head. "Nope. Pretend I didn't say that. Next topic please!"

"You do realize that both of us have perfect recall and will never forget you said that?" Wreckage asked, grinning now.

"I'm choosing to ignore that fact." Jade pointed in the direction they'd been heading before they'd gotten distracted. "Where's this restaurant we're going to?"

"Not far. End of this block and to the right. Just long enough for you to answer a question for me," Ruin said.

"Fair enough. Ask me anything not related to my last statement that I am totally pretending I didn't make."

"What was it like on Earth?"

The question surprised her, but the answer came easily. "Like living in a prison for your entire life without ever knowing what you'd done wrong. Athens Two wasn't even the worst of the hive cities. In fact, I've heard from others it was one of the better ones."

They walked as she described the place she'd come from. "Earth is a hellscape outside the hives. We poisoned the oceans and the atmosphere. There are stories about a huge explosion destroying a swath of the planet. Some say it was an asteroid, and others claim it was a super volcano. I've even heard tales that an ancient power reactor blew up. I'm sure someone knows the truth, but no one in the hives really worried about it. We were focused on making it through another day. There wasn't time to think about the past."

"And you never saw the sun?" Wreckage asked.

"I saw it a few times. Even went outside once or twice when I was a kid. We found air vents that led outside, to the gap between the walls of the hive and the energy barriers that protected us from the storms and toxic atmosphere."

"Your life wasn't that much different from ours," Ruin murmured.

"We were all victims of the corporations," she agreed. "Though we had some protections that you didn't. We weren't born into service. We had to apply for the chance to be indentured servants. The corporations treated the hive cities like factories that produced workers as the product. They sorted through the inventory and picked out the ones they wanted. The rest of us were left to fend for ourselves."

"Why didn't any of the corporations select you?" Wreckage asked. "You would have been an asset to them."

She made a derisive noise. "Because I never applied. By the time I was old enough to qualify, I'd already scrounged and bartered enough to get my first implants. I knew what path I wanted, and it didn't involve working for a *fraxxing* corporation." That had been Marco's choice, and she'd never understood why he'd done it.

"Do you still have any family left on Earth?" Ruin asked.

"None. My parents died when I was still a girl. My oldest brother, Marco, took care of us for a while, but when he came of age, he signed on with Bellex Corporation and left us behind. My other brother died of an overdose about a year later. Maggie is my family now. We made it out together."

"Like us," Wreckage said, his voice soft.

"Only the two of you *are* brothers. You stuck together and survived. My family didn't." Then she realized what she'd said and blanched. "I'm sorry. That came out wrong. You lost the rest of your batch-siblings in the wars. That means you're alone now, too. I didn't mean to dismiss your loss."

Wreckage's expression turned stormy for a moment, and she got the feeling he was about to say something important, but Ruin spoke up first.

"The important thing is that none of us are alone tonight," he stated, his tone firm. "And that's our destination up ahead."

The restaurant wasn't at all what she'd expected. The name had conjured images of dim booths and soft, sultry music. Instead, the place was bright and cheery. Large murals adorned the walls, each one titled to indicate it was a scene from some area of Earth. If that was true, they had to be centuries out of date because the planet definitely didn't look like that anymore. A gold-skinned Vardarian female greeted them just inside the door. She wore a human-style dress tailored to accommodate her wings and wore a *harani* on her bicep. "Welcome to our establishment. I'm Gali, one of the owners. How many are in your party?"

"Three," Wreckage replied. "And please say hello to Zena for us."

Gali brightened. "You can greet her yourself. She'll be your server tonight." The Vardarian lowered her voice. "We're still teaching her how to cook."

Wreckage burst out laughing, and even Ruin grinned. "Good luck with that."

"I can hear you!" another female voice called from the back. A tall, athletically built woman with shoulder-length brown hair stepped into view. She was dressed much like Gali, down to the *harani* she wore on her arm. Since she wasn't one of the handful of humans on the planet, Jade knew she was a cyborg. One she hadn't met yet.

"I was teasing, my *mahaya*," Gali said as Zena approached.

"I know, love." Zena winked at her mate. "I'll show our guests to their table. You better warn Inet that we've got a couple of cyborgs out here."

"I'll break out the big plates," Gali said with a smile.

Wreckage clapped his hands together eagerly. "That's what I like to hear."

The menu was the most eclectic combination of dishes Jade had ever seen. Some were familiar, like cheeseburgers or pizza, but others were entirely new to her. She read descriptions for things called kebabs, empanadas, tacos, and other items. They all sounded delicious, but she decided to try one she knew and see how two aliens and a cyborg interpreted a cheeseburger.

They all ordered milkshakes and their meals. Jade watched the three women laugh and flirt with each other as they worked. They were happy, and it showed in everything they did. If the food was decent, she'd be back here again soon.

Once they had their drinks, they started conversing again. "How was your first day of work?" Wreckage asked.

Her answer came easily, her hands fluttering in front of her as she tried to convey her thoughts. "It was fantastic. Phaedra set up this amazing rig for me. It's not quite the same as being jacked in, but it was closer than I ever imagined I'd get. My teammates are friendly and competent, and the palace is like no place I've ever seen. It's busy and quiet at the same time. Like, there's a serious hush over the place, but everyone was nice and welcoming."

Both men relaxed. "So, you're staying here?" Ruin asked.

She reached across the table to take their hands, her next words already framed in her mind. "I'm staying. Why wouldn't I? I have everything I want right here."

"So do we," Wreckage said.

Ruin didn't say anything, but he curled his large hand around her smaller one and nodded.

This was the start of something good. She could feel it. Now all she had to do was hold on to it as long as she could.

6

———

THE NEXT FEW days were almost too perfect to believe. She split her time between her new job and spending time with Ruin and Wreckage. They went out for dinners, strolled through the artists' district, and shopped in the market. They bought small gifts for each other, all of them intended to make the others laugh. They talked and got to know each other, and with every passing day, the chemistry between them grew hotter.

Her new job was challenging enough to keep her interested and made the time at work fly by. Phaedra accompanied her into cyberspace, showing her the intricate security systems and layers of defenses that protected the planet and everything orbiting it.

It still felt strange to be inside a system without having hacked her way in, but it came with the ability to do so much more than she'd ever dared to do when she was an intruder. She tried to hack her way inside a few times, too. She'd done it once before when the mercs holding her prisoner had forced her to, but the access she'd used back then wasn't available anymore. In fact, she only found one way inside the system, and once she'd tagged it, she and the others had worked together to close the security gap.

Each morning, she'd find a present on her doorstep. Usually it would be flowers, but once it was a pair of hammered copper cuffs that fit over her wrists and hid her scars. She wore them every day and smiled every time she looked down at her hands.

On the fourth day, everything changed.

Phaedra had invited her to attend the throne room when the announcement about her baby was made. Many of the staff were there, along with the ruling council of Haven. The entire speech would be broadcast live to the rest of the colony, ensuring everyone heard the news at the same time.

Jade had asked if Wreckage and Ruin could come as her guests, and Phaedra had happily agreed. "The more the merrier," she'd said.

It was their first daytime date, and it felt like a milestone. It also helped to have them both here in case things went badly after the announcement. She always felt safer when she was with them. In fact, she'd never had an episode when they were around.

Now, Jade stood between the two massive cyborgs and watched as her friend and employer stood on a dais, flanked by her *mahoyen*. Prince Tyran looked regal and stalwart while Braxon kept one hand on Phaedra's shoulder and the other resting close to the hilt of the knife on his belt.

Phaedra turned and whispered something to Braxon, who shuffled his feet and did his best to relax.

"They're prepared for trouble," Ruin noted.

"Whatever they're about to say, it's going to cause problems." Wreckage glanced down at her. "Isn't it?"

Jade nodded. She hadn't told them what today's announcement was about. It wasn't her secret to reveal. "Maybe."

The two cyborgs moved in closer, both of them tense and on alert. Jade didn't expect anything to happen right away. In her heart, she hoped nothing happened at all and everyone accepted this decision. This was a personal choice by Phaedra and her mates and should be respected as such.

The prince spoke first, addressing everyone in the colony. While he was the official founder of the colony and the leader of the Vardarians who lived here, he never acted as if his word was law. He sat on the leadership council with the others and they made decisions together, always trying to do what was best for the colony as a whole.

He was a charismatic speaker, drawing the crowd in as he talked about the future of the colony. New buildings were under construction, more colonists would be arriving from Earth in a matter of weeks, and a human doctor had been hired and was expected to set up shop shortly. That last bit intrigued Jade. Would the new doctor have knowledge that would increase her chances of getting some of her implants back online?

Tyran put his arm across Phaedra's shoulders so his hand lay over Braxon's forearm, linking the three of them in the eyes of everyone watching. "You all know that Haven was founded to be a place where all of us could escape the ever-tightening noose of tradition. In keeping with that premise, we have made a decision."

He paused for a perfectly timed moment before continuing. "As you know, our *mahaya* will soon give birth to our first child. We have decided that our baby will not undergo the traditional genetic manipulations to ensure they are pure Vardarian. They will be the first Vardarian-human hybrid born on this planet. It is our hope they will not be the last."

"Whoa," Wreckage murmured.

"Yeah. Is this why they brought you onto the team? So you can help protect the princess from whatever comes next?" Ruin asked.

Jade nodded. She was proud of her new role but also worried about what might happen now the word was out. "That's part of the reason. Not to mention Phaedra's due date is coming up. She needs to take care of herself and her plus one. I had no idea how exhausting it was growing another person."

Wreckage shot her an amused look. "I've never

heard it put quite that way before. You make it sound like hard work."

"Being a parent *is* hard work. It's physically and emotionally demanding. You don't get time off, and the work contract is at least fifteen years."

Neither of them replied, and she wondered if she'd said something to upset them. *Fraxx.* Did they want kids? Were they yearning for a family? If they were, that might be a big fraxxing issue. She didn't want children. She wanted to be free to live her life any way she wanted. If she had kids, their needs would come first.

A murmur in the surrounding crowd drew her thoughts back to the here and now. Whispers raced through the crowd, heads bowed, and people huddled together to share their reactions. Most of them smiled and nodded but not everyone. To her shock, one of the ones looking unhappy was her teammate, Allax. His scales gleamed as if he was agitated or about to attack, and his expression was distinctly unhappy.

She made a note to warn Phaedra about him. It was probably nothing to worry about, but it was worth mentioning. Just in case.

Ruin heard everything Jade said, but thanks to his enhanced senses, he also caught a great deal more. Her micro-expressions told him this was a strongly held opinion, and her voice held almost inaudible undertones of guilt and determination.

He wished they were somewhere private so they could talk about it. He could tell her they weren't looking to have children, either. In fact, they were on fertility blockers to ensure they remained childless. They had more than enough family already... which was another conversation they needed to have, and soon.

Fraxx. So far, this relationship required too much talking about things he'd rather never discuss again. As much as he wanted Jade in their lives, he wasn't sure it was worth the cost. More than just his life could be upended if the truth got out. It would affect too many of the cyborgs in the colony.

A quick scan of the room showed him that several cyborgs were present, including River, Edge, and Thrash. One of these days, someone would notice. Every time they came into town increased the odds of discovery. He wasn't ready for that... but he wasn't ready to give up Jade, either. They had to find another way.

A small reception followed the speech, but Jade convinced them to leave early so she could show them her workplace. Ruin was just relieved to get out of the crowded room. Places like this always reminded him of the times he'd been packed into a shuttle's hold before a deployment or the holding pens that were only used when they had VIPs coming through on their pointless inspections.

"And this is me," Jade's comment snapped him out of his dark thoughts.

"The chair floats?" Wreckage asked.

"It does. And it follows my movements so I can rotate and position it however I want. That's why it feels so much like being jacked in. In the datasphere I can fly through the data, literally. It's the most amazing feeling, and I never thought I'd get to experience it again. This makes it possible. It's not the same, but it's close."

He wanted to say something supportive, but what came out was something else. "And when you're in the datasphere, how safe are you from attack?"

The light in Jade's eyes dimmed a little. "As safe as we can be, but if there's a security breach, that's on us. We're the ones tasked with protecting Liberty and everyone on it."

"So you're taking Phaedra's place on the front line because she's a target now?" he asked.

"You already asked me that, and the answer is the same. She's a target, yes. And she's also very pregnant and needs to take care of herself." Jade lifted her chin and glared up at him. "I can take care of myself. This is what I'm good at. It might be all I'm good at."

"That's not true," Wreckage protested.

"It's also irrelevant to this conversation." Ruin's temper was rising, and he didn't understand why. Part of him knew he needed to shut up, but his mouth kept running on autopilot.

Wreckage shook his head sharply in warning, and Jade set her hands on her hips.

"My life. My job. My choice. None of it is *irrelevant*," she stated.

"When you were on Earth, you had to do this to survive. You had no choice. Now, you can be anything you want. Do anything you want. Something safer. We can't protect you in there."

"I can protect myself. That's not what I want from you, Ru." She'd never called him that before, and it was almost enough to derail his sudden, senseless anger.

Almost.

"Then what do you want from me?" he asked.

Jade threw up her hands. "I thought it was pretty obvious. I want you. Your time. Your company. I don't want a bodyguard. I want *you*." She glanced at Wreckage. "Both of you."

"I took that as a given," Wreckage said and then turned to glower at Ruin. "Though right now I'm not sure why you'd want to spend time with this cranky *bakaffa*. What is wrong with you, Ruin?"

"Too much time in town. Too many people." He dragged a hand through his hair and growled in frustration. "I'm not sure I can do this. I need to get out of here. I'm sorry."

He walked away, already regretting the entire fiasco and wondering what the *fraxx* was wrong with him. Why was he so angry, and why couldn't he control it?

The moment he reached the palace gate, he broke into a run, leaving his hover-bike behind. He'd come back to for it later. Right now, he needed to blow off some steam before he made things worse.

Wreckage watched his batch-brother storm away. He hadn't seen Ruin like this since before they'd arrived at Haven. As prisoners, they'd both had their share of struggles and dark days, but Ruin's moods could get dangerously dark. When that happened, he'd lash out in anger, which usually resulted in beatings and other punishments.

He didn't know what had triggered this bout of anger, but he'd have to wait to talk to his brother about it. If he went after him now, it would just piss the big idiot off even more.

"What just happened?" Jade asked, pain and confusion thickening her voice.

"Ruin just lived up to his name." Wreckage tried to make it a joke, but it fell flat. "He's broken, Jade. Just like you and me. This happens sometimes. He'll get over it."

"I don't even know what he needs to get over. What did I do?"

"Nothing. It wasn't you." Wreckage wrapped an

arm around her waist and pulled her up against him. She came to him willingly, which made him relax a little. Whatever damage Ruin had just done, it wasn't total.

"Then why?" she asked.

"He's as broken as the rest of us, sweetling. He just doesn't deal with it very well."

Jade pressed her face into his shirt and laughed softly, the sound only a little bitter. "You can say that again. I've never seen him like that."

"I have. It's been a while, though. He's been better since we came here."

"So, what do you think changed?"

He had his suspicions about that, but this wasn't the time or the place to discuss it. This had to be a conversation between the three of them, and it would be best to wait until Ruin was in a better mind-set. He chose his next words carefully. "I think you're important to him and he doesn't want anything to happen to you. We've lost too many people we cared about already."

Jade lifted her head to look up at him. "You're telling me that he was a jerk because he cares about me?"

"Afraid so, sweetling." He kissed the tip of her nose, smiled, and threw his batch-brother under the mass transport vehicle. "The big, bad cyborg is having big feelings and doesn't know how to deal with it."

She snickered and then laughed and hugged him.

"You better hope he's out of earshot or he's going to be *really* pissed that you said that."

"Probably, but that doesn't mean it isn't true. Remember when we warned you that we'd never dated anyone before? This is us trying to figure shit out as we go. No doubt I'll screw up soon, and Ruin will be with you, explaining to you why I'm an idiot."

Jade laughed again, and he felt her tension melt away. "What have I gotten myself into?"

"No comment," was all he said. "Now, does part of this tour include giving me a demonstration of what it's like inside cyberspace?"

"Is this a real request or are you trying to distract me from what happened with Ruin?" she asked.

"A little of both," he admitted. "I really am curious, though. I imagined it would just be you surrounded by squiggly lines of data that no one else can read."

She snorted with laughter and pulled him to her chair. "Luckily, this thing is built for anything up to and including Torski physiology. Sit down and strap in."

"And if I do that, where will you sit?" He tried to sound casual, but by all the stars in the galaxy, he knew exactly where he wanted her to be.

The smile she shot him confirmed his wish was about to come true. "In your lap. You don't mind. Do you?"

He dropped into the chair and immediately patted his thighs. "Show me what you've got, sweetling."

Jade helped him with the unfamiliar harness and then snuggled into his lap, clipping herself to him with a few extra straps so both of them were secure.

"Once I bring up the holographic display, you'll see everything from my point of view. Think of yourself as a passenger inside a tour shuttle. You can't interact, but you can look at everything."

"Works for me." He relaxed into the chair and just enjoyed the chance to hold her in his arms.

Then the display activated, and he was transported to a digital wonderland that took his breath away. It was all the more amazing because Jade was his guide, showing him the world she loved. The experience confirmed what he'd already begun to realize. They needed to end their self-imposed exile. If they didn't, they'd miss out on too many things and too many important moments with the ones they cared about.

7

───────

RUIN TOOK the long way home, running for almost an hour before he finally reached the cabin. He went inside just long enough to change into his work clothes, grabbed his tools, and started to peel the logs they'd need to expand the cabin.

The weather was as unsettled as he felt. The wind was damp and ruffled, the sky a constant parade of clouds that marched across the sun. His anger had faded, leaving him confused and frustrated with himself. He regretted the way he'd spoken to Jade. *Fraxx*, he regretted everything that had happened since the prince's speech.

The harder he worked, the clearer his mind got, but he still couldn't put his finger on what had triggered his fit of temper. He owed Jade an apology. He probably owed Wreckage one, too.

He stopped working and looked around as it

finally dawned on him that Wreckage wasn't back yet. Was he still with Jade? The thought hit him with a jolt of envy, followed by guilt. Getting jealous of Wreckage was pointless. They were in this together. Weren't they?

"Hey, asshole. Is it safe to approach?" Wreckage sent through their link.

"Yeah. It's safe." Ruin made a show of putting down his tools and raising his hands so his brother could see them. "Get over here so you can tell me what a dumbass I am."

Wreckage walked out of the woods and made his way over. "Dumbass doesn't begin to describe you. I made a list on the way over here. Want to hear it?"

"Not really."

"I even sorted it alphabetically. It starts with asshole."

Ruin sighed. "So does mine. How is she?"

"Our little goddess is confused and hurt, no thanks to you." Wreckage folded his arms and scowled at him. "She thought you were calling the whole thing off."

"I wasn't. If I were going to do that, I'd find a better way."

"I know that. You know that. Jade didn't. All you said was that you couldn't do this and then stormed out." Then Wreckage registered the last bit, and his scowl deepened. "*If* you were going to? What, break it off? Why would you do that?"

Ruin   snarled   as   frustration   rendered   him

temporarily speechless, and Wreckage took a step back.

"Whoa. Take a breath. Hell, take several. Then I need you to tell me what's going on."

He took two deep breaths and shook his shoulders to try and loosen them. "Do you remember why we decided to live out here?"

"Because we wanted to put some distance between us and the other cyborgs." Wreckage gestured around them. "And because we're happier out here in the woods. It's easier."

"It is. But lately we've been spending a lot of time in town."

"Because that's where Jade is." Wreckage's expression turned guarded. "You were serious. You're thinking of walking away from her?"

"I don't know. I don't want to, but today..." Ruin cursed, leaned over, and grabbed a branch from a pile to hurl it through the air like a spear.

"The speech. Lots of people crowded together, no easy way out." Wreckage nodded in understanding. "I felt it too. But not the way you did. Why didn't you say something?"

"I didn't realize at the time. Did you see who else was there?"

"Edge, River, and Thrash. Of course they attended. Edge and River are on the council. River wants out, though, so they're bringing Thrash up as a possible replacement."

"River's a good leader. She should stay."

"You know she won't. She's still struggling with the discovery of the sleeper codes the Grays installed without her knowledge. She doesn't trust herself right now. I'd feel the same way."

"But Thrash?" Ruin still couldn't imagine the young cyborg as a leader.

"He's changed. He's not the same headstrong idiot he was while we were prisoners."

Ruin raised a brow. "You sure about that? He was the one running the betting pool on *our* dating life just a few days ago."

Wreckage guffawed and raised a hand. "Point taken. But better him than either of us."

"Truth." Ruin blew out a breath and felt his mind settle a bit. "This is harder than I expected." The confession caught him by surprise.

"Yeah. I figured. To be honest, I'm finding it easier than I thought it would be. But this only works if we're both committed. She wants both of us. Though why she's so keen on an asshole like you is anyone's guess."

"It's my charm and good looks," Ruin shot back. "You're the pity date."

"I'm pretty sure you have that backward." Wreckage punched him lightly in the arm. "So, what now? How do we make this work? I guess a better question is, do you want this to work?"

"I do." The answer came so quickly it had to be

true. Despite his doubts and issues, he didn't want to give up Jade.

"Good. If you were thinking about walking away, I was going to have to beat some sense into you, and that might take weeks."

"I can't spend so much time in town. It puts me on edge and... well, we saw what happens when I'm wound up."

"Okay. But we'll have to explain that to Jade." Wreckage pinched his chin in thought for a few seconds and then smiled. "What if we started spending time with her one on one? She took me into cyberspace today, just the two of us, and it was amazing. I can take her into town, and during your time maybe the two of you can go for walks along the river or take one of the hover-bikes and show her the area. Did you know she's never been more than a mile away from the colony? Maggie's taken her into the woods a few times, but they never go far."

"When did you get so smart?" Ruin liked the idea. The woods were where he felt most at peace. Sharing that part of him with Jade felt right.

"I was always the smart one. You were just in denial. Is that your way of agreeing with my plan?"

"It is." He slapped Wreckage's arm hard enough to send the other cyborg staggering. "Thank you. And thanks for staying with Jade after I left. I'm glad you were there for her."

"You still need to apologize to her."

"Yeah. And speaking of that, I'm sorry I walked out and left you to deal with the fallout. I wasn't thinking."

"No, you were reacting. But I get it."

They lapsed into silence for several long minutes. Finally, Ruin cleared his throat. "We're going to have to talk to her about…"

"Yeah. We are. But not yet. We're already over the drama limit for the day, and we still need to get ready for tonight."

"Tonight? What's happening tonight?" Ruin wanted to see Jade again, but the thought of going back into town wasn't appealing.

Wreckage gave him a shit-eating grin that told him to brace for impact. "Oh, didn't I tell you? Jade's coming over for dinner tonight. Since you left your hover-bike at the palace, I figured I'd drop you off and you could bring her back with you."

"Jade's coming here? Tonight?" Ruin looked around the mess he'd made of the yard and then thought about the state of their cabin. "*Fraxxing* hell! I'll start out here. You tackle the cabin. And the food. Veth, what are we feeding her?"

"Relax. I already messaged Anya. She and Saral are putting together a takeout meal for the three of us. I'll grab it while you get Jade."

"Nice of you to make a plan without consulting me."

"You needed some alone time to deal with your

shit. Now suck it up and get moving. We have a lot of work to do."

Jade assumed Wreckage would be the one to pick her up, but when she opened the door of her apartment, Ruin stood there.

"Hi."

"Hello, little goddess." To her shock, he dropped onto one knee in front of her. "I'm sorry. I was an asshole today and I regret what I did."

"Uh. Wow. That... is the best apology I've ever heard." She floundered for something meaningful to say, but she was too surprised.

"It was?" Ruin looked up at her and smiled a little. "It's not something I do often. I had to rehearse it on my way here."

She laughed and bent down to hug him. "It was a lovely apology, and I'm glad you're sorry. Next time you feel like that, will you tell me instead of getting mad?"

"I didn't know I was angry until it all spilled over." He looked lost and more than a little embarrassed by the admission. She'd never seen him like this, and it made her like him more than ever.

"I know how that can be. I get like that sometimes if something happens that reminds me of my time with the mercenaries. I get all wound up and can't breathe.

Sometimes it makes me mad. Other times I get so scared I can't move."

"My behavioral programming defaults to anger every time. Scared soldiers don't fight as well as angry ones." He swallowed and wrapped his arms around her. "Do you forgive me?"

"Of course I do. I'm just glad you're here. I thought maybe..." she trailed off, unwilling to finish the statement.

"You thought I was done. Wreck told me. We are not done, little goddess. In fact, we're only just getting started. That's what tonight is about."

"Good," she didn't bother hiding the relief in her voice. "I take it we need to make some changes?"

He got to his feet while keeping her in his arms. "A few. I'll explain on the way. This has nothing to do with you, Jade. This is about me."

She looked up at him and smiled. "It's about *us*."

Flying on a hover-bike was almost as good as soaring through cyberspace. The wind buffeted her body and roared past them loudly enough to be heard inside her helmet. She sat behind Ruin, their bodies pressed together and her arms locked tightly around his waist. She didn't have to do that since they were both wearing harnesses. But why waste a chance to snuggle up with him?

He talked as they flew, occasionally interrupting his explanation of what happened that day to point out various landmarks. She could actually feel him relax as they flew away from Haven, and by the time he set down near their cabin, she understood things better.

His triggers were different from hers, and his reactions weren't the same either, but the underlying issue was the same. Their experiences affected how they dealt with the present, and sometimes they couldn't control the results.

Ruin dismounted first and then lifted her off the bike and set her down beside him. She removed her helmet and handed it to him, looking around her the whole time.

A breeze blew through the clearing, carrying the scents of the forest. She had no idea what they were, other than the deep, loamy smell of the dirt beneath her feet and the sharper scent of freshly cut wood. The wind in the trees made a constant, whispering noise that reminded her of the ventilation system in Athens Two, though the air here was so clean and clear it surprised her each time she drew a deep breath.

The cabin was solid and welcoming, despite the fact it was made entirely from trees instead of the usual building materials. Peeled logs stacked atop each other formed a surprisingly large building with warm lights glowing from the windows.

"Welcome to our home," Ruin murmured, his hand resting on the small of her back as he guided her past a stack of partially peeled logs.

"You built this yourself. Didn't you?"

"We did. And we're expanding it now that the

weather is good again. By the time winter comes, this place will be as nice as any home in the colony."

"How?" she asked, curious.

"We're using solar power to charge up a bank of batteries so we have power. There's a deep well out back and we hired a Vardarian plumber to draw up the plans and a guide so we could set it up ourselves."

"I can't wait to see inside." She'd imagined they led a far more rustic life than this, and now her curiosity was piqued.

"Come with me and we'll give you the tour."

The interior was another surprise. The log walls were left uncovered in some places, but in others, it was impossible to tell she wasn't standing in any of the mass-built homes in the colony. The walls were relatively bare of art or other personal items, but that was hardly surprising given who lived here. She'd discovered that most of the cyborgs were minimalists.

The kitchen was the one area that lacked some modern amenities. A basic cooling unit sat across the room from an object she'd never seen outside of historical vids. "Is that a wood-burning stove?"

Wreckage looked up from the counter where he'd been laying out the night's meal. "It is. Good for soups and stews and burning everything else we try to cook on it."

"Which is why tonight's dinner is from the Bar None." Ruin pointed to the familiar logo on the takeout containers that littered the counter.

Jade wandered into the main room that took up most of the cabin. Huge, overstuffed chairs sat near the window and a more sensibly sized sofa sat against one wall. One of the shorter walls looked empty and unfinished. "What's supposed to go there?" she asked.

"A fireplace. Not that we'll need the heat, but we decided that if we're going to live in a cabin in the woods, we had to have a fireplace," Wreckage said.

"It sounds cozy. We used to light fires sometimes down in the lower levels to stay warm. It was forbidden of course. It was a terrible waste of oxygen and resources, but we did it anyway."

"I thought it was warmer underground?" Ruin asked.

"It was. But the parts of the tower above ground needed to be heated, so the warmer air was constantly being vented upward and the cooler air sent down to be heated. In summer we were always hot and in winter we froze, all so the upper levels could be comfortable."

Ruin moved in behind her, his arms snaking around her waist to pull her back against his body. "You'll never freeze with us around. We can control our body temperature. If you ever get the slightest bit chilly, you can snuggle up with one of us."

"Or both," Wreckage added.

Visions of her snuggled between the two cyborgs filled her mind. They started off innocently, but within seconds she was imagining the three of them naked and doing things that would keep them warm for hours.

She'd come out here because she wanted to see how they lived, but now she was here, it occurred to her that neither of them had mentioned taking her back to town tonight.

Were they hoping she'd stay? What would she say if they asked?

Jade leaned back into Ruin's embrace and closed her eyes. She felt safe, warm, and cherished—the way she always did when the three of them were together.

Why would she go when everything she wanted was right here in this cabin?

8

———

Dinner passed in a genial blur of good food and easy conversation. Considering the day's events, tonight could have gone another way, but the three of them had managed to navigate their first *fraxx*-up. Wreckage had no illusions it would be their last, but hopefully the next one would be a long time coming.

Jade insisted on helping clean up afterward, which was something new and made him consider that they might need to increase the size of that room, too.

"Tell me more about this idea for separate dates," she asked while Ruin washed and she dried the night's dishes.

Wreckage was breaking down the containers and scraps for recycling and waited for Ruin to answer. This should come from him.

"It was Wreckage's idea. He pointed out that we've

only dated you together. That's not wrong, but it would be nice to have some time alone with you, too."

"I like the idea, but I don't want this to become a love triangle type situation. I like spending time with both of you together."

Ruin nodded and handed her another plate, his suds-covered hand brushing over Jade's in a tender gesture that made Wreckage smile. His batch-brother could be as smooth as *keski* silk when he wasn't being an idiot.

"Town is..." Ruin made a noise somewhere between a grunt and a huff. "I get wound up if I'm there too often. I thought you and I could explore the woods a bit. Maybe take the hover-bike out for a day trip."

"The woods?" Jade perked up. "Maggie has been trying to get me out into nature, but she's been so busy at work we haven't had a lot of time for it since the weather improved. She also stressed it wasn't entirely safe out there, so I shouldn't go alone."

"That's because she nearly got attacked by a bark spider while she was wandering around out there. If Striker hadn't been there, she'd have died," Wreckage said.

"Yeah, she used that as an example of the dangers out there. But the two of you are rangers, and you live out here. I'd be safe with you."

Ruin shot him a satisfied look. Protecting her was a privilege neither of them wanted to give up.

"You are always safe with us, little goddess," Ruin said.

Jade's eyes gleamed with sudden mischief. "That's good since I agreed to come out to your cabin in the middle of the woods for dinner. That's not something I would have ever done back at the hive. I mean, here I am, alone with two dangerous cyborgs who could do anything they wanted to me, and no one is around to overhear or interrupt us."

Was she flirting with them? Or suggesting...

Ruin sent him a message. *"Did that mean what I think it meant?"*

"I think so. Hell, I hope so."

Tonight's invitation was intended to let them speak openly and honestly about matters, not about getting her alone for other reasons. But they had talked things out, and she was still here. Fraxx it. He needed to know what she was thinking.

"What kind of things would someone passing by hear, exactly?" he asked.

Jade dried off her hands with slow, deliberate motions, her eyes fixed on her task. "I guess that depends on what happens next." She paused, took a soft breath, and then added, "And whether I'm going home tonight, or tomorrow morning."

Ruin still had soap suds on his hands when he turned and pulled her into his arms. "You're staying."

She laughed, scooped a handful of the creamy

white foam out of the sink, and flicked it at him. "Is that a request or a command?"

He blew the suds away from his mouth and grinned at her. "Both. Either. Whichever one you're most likely to agree to."

Part of him wanted to join in this moment, but Wreckage stayed where he was. He'd never seen Ruin like this. Eager, playful, and *happy*.

"Hmm. I like that answer. So my answer is yes. If you can catch me." Jade spun and ducked out of Ruin's arms, somehow managing to catch him with a handful of soapy water as she danced out of reach.

Ruin spluttered, water running down his face and his beard full of bubbles.

Jade took another step backward, still laughing, so focused on keeping her distance from Ruin that she forgot about Wreckage.

A mistake he was more than happy to take advantage of.

He caught her from behind and lifted her into the air. "We're going to have to work on your situational awareness, sweetling."

She yelped and made a half-hearted attempt to break out of his hold. "*Veth*! I didn't think this through. I'm outnumbered." She didn't sound at all unhappy about being caught.

"What should we do with the little minx?" Ruin asked, his smile almost predatory.

"Well, she did get you wet," Wreckage observed. "I think we should do the same to her."

"Just a reminder, I only have one set of clothes with me. Unless you want to fly me home tomorrow morning naked or in one of your shirts, do not wreck my outfit."

"Us wreck something?" Wreckage teased.

"Or ruin it?" Ruin chimed in.

"Why would you think such a thing?"

"Maggie warned me cyborgs were hard on clothes. Striker keeps tearing hers off."

"She *told* you that?" Ruin asked.

"Well, yeah. Best friends have no secrets."

"That explains a lot," Wreckage agreed. If the women of the colony regularly shared that kind of information, what else were they talking about?

"Indeed." Ruin met his gaze. "Which means we need to provide our little goddess with an impressive tale to tell the others tomorrow."

He felt Jade shiver and heard the way her breath caught in her throat. She was eager for what they had planned for her.

So was he.

His cock was hard enough to pound hull plating and his blood burned like it was on fire. Every time Jade moved, her body ground against his, teasing him mercilessly.

"*Shower?*" Ruin sent the one-word message through their link.

"*Shower*," Wreckage confirmed.

Without a word, they both left the kitchen. Ruin stripped off his shirt as he walked while Wreckage managed to get his arm under Jade's legs so she was cradled against his chest.

"Uh. Where are we going?" she asked.

Neither of them answered.

"Guys? Hello?"

"Trust us, sweetling. We will never dish out a punishment you don't enjoy as much as we do."

Her soft gasp of anticipation was one of the most beautiful sounds he'd ever heard. He wanted to hear it again, so he bowed his head over hers, brushing a soft kiss to her hairline as he murmured his next words. "We're going to make you scream with pleasure until you beg us to fuck you. You're ours now."

This time, her gasp was accompanied by a low, needy sound that nearly brought him to his knees.

"*Fraxx*," Wreckage groaned. "Do you know how sexy you sound?"

The little minx smirked. "Maybe."

Ruin turned and held out his arms. His pants were undone and barely clung to his hips, which meant Wreckage had some catching up to do. "Give her to me."

Wreckage handed her over and then bent down to kiss her hard. "Behave. Ruin isn't as patient as I am."

"Then you better hurry," Jade said.

Their little goddess was hotter than a supernova when she got sassy.

He moved past Ruin, already skinning his shirt over his head as he jogged the last few meters to the bathroom.

The time for talking was over.

"So, you're the impatient one?" Jade asked. She hadn't planned on things happening this way, but once again, her mouth had engaged before her brain. Usually, that got her in trouble. Tonight, it got her exactly what she wanted.

"I can be." Ruin's voice was a low rumble that rolled through her smaller frame. "But only when I don't get what I want."

She placed her hand on his bare chest, tracing the line of his collarbone with one finger. Her hand shook as she spoke. "I think we're all going to get what we want. I've dreamed about this so many times, but I never thought it would be more than that. I know I'm damaged goods."

"Look at me." It wasn't a request but a command, one that made her stomach flutter and her pussy grow wet with need. She looked into his eyes. "My doubts were never about you. When I look at you, I see a strong, determined survivor, and the most beautiful woman on this whole planet. You deserve better than someone like me. I've done things..."

She shook her head and then moved in to kiss him, sealing his mouth before he could say anything else.

He groaned, arms flexing as he lifted her higher and took control of their kiss. His mouth was a brand against her skin, his beard rasping against her cheek. When his tongue swept past her lips, she moaned at the new sensation, her mouth opening to his.

The sound of running water registered in the back of her mind, but she didn't pay attention until a waft of steam drifted into the hallway.

Ruin moved without breaking their kiss, carrying her not into one of their bedrooms but to the bathroom.

Confused, she raised her head to look around. "We're not going to bed?"

"We'll get there eventually. First, we promised to get you wet," Wreckage said.

She turned to look at him and caught an eyeful of hard muscle and bare skin. He'd stripped completely in the time he'd been gone, and the sight momentarily cost her the ability to speak.

Steam swirled around him, water glistening on his golden skin. His hair was wet and slicked back, and she realized he stood inside the largest shower she'd ever seen.

Unlike the rest of the house, everything about this room was modern. The floor tiles were gray and black stone while the tiles on the walls were white and gray.

The fixtures were white with soft, fluffy towels folded neatly beside the door to the massive shower. Clear glass enclosed the space, which was more than large enough to accommodate the three of them.

"You like getting clean that much?" she asked, gesturing at the massive enclosure and the gorgeous man standing inside it.

"Showering with unlimited amounts of hot water is something we never experienced until we came here," Ruin explained.

"So this is the one room where we indulged ourselves when planning this place," Wreckage said.

"And now I get to indulge in it with you." She let her gaze move over Wreckage's naked body.

"Not yet. We need to do one more thing first." Wreckage prowled toward her, his erection bobbing as he moved.

Ruin set her down on the floor and immediately started to undo the fastenings down the front of her top.

Wreckage stopped in front, kissed her softly, and then traced his hands up her thighs until they reached her waistband. He drew her pants down slowly, revealing the only frivolous and frilly pair of panties she owned. They were red and lacy, and she'd bought them because she'd never seen anything so luxurious.

"You've been keeping secrets." Wreckage pulled her pants down until they were on her thighs.

"Ruin, look at what she's been hiding from us."

She felt Ruin shift his body so he could look down over her shoulder. A moment later he growled her name, one hand leaving her shirt to slide down her front until his big hand cupped her mons. "Pretty. But not as pretty as what's beneath."

He slipped two fingers under the thin lace and into her pussy. She didn't bother to muffle the moan that rose from her throat. It felt too good, and all she wanted was more.

"You're already wet for us," he whispered approvingly.

"Strip her the rest of the way, Wreck. Our goddess needs to be worshiped properly."

"For the record, I'm only doing what you said because I like your plan, not because you told me to."

Wreckage's retort made Jade laugh, but it changed to a groan a second later as Ruin ran the pad of his finger over her throbbing clit.

"I think she liked that. Do it again," Wreckage suggested.

Ruin locked one arm around her to support her while he fucked her with his fingers. She leaned against him, trusting him to hold her. Trusting him to give her all the pleasure she craved while Wreckage undressed her. She'd never given up control like this before. It was profoundly addictive to let it all go and still feel safe and loved... She scrubbed that word out of her head the moment it appeared. That way lay potential heartache and a whole mess of problems she wasn't ready for. Better to stay in the moment. Especially when the moment was so *fraxxing* good.

Ruin's hand sped up, creating a delicious friction that made her quiver and buck against him. The closer he brought her to orgasm, the louder she moaned, encouraging him to keep going, to give her what she needed.

Just as she teetered on the brink, he stopped. "Not yet. When you come, it will be with one of us inside you. Not before."

"But... I..." she panted out the words, every part of her screaming with need.

"You need to wait until I've had a taste. Soon, sweetling. We'll let you come soon." Wreckage stood up and gathered her into his arms as Ruin stepped back. She heard the rustle of fabric and realized he was getting out of his pants. He'd nearly brought her to orgasm before getting naked. She was in the best kind of trouble right now.

"This way," Wreckage walked her into the middle of the shower, so they both stood beneath the cascade of hot water. It fell like rain, soothing and sensuous as it flowed over her skin.

They washed her together, batting away her hands each time she tried to do the same for them.

"Let us take care of you," Ruin said.

They were giving her another chance to let go, and she took it happily.

Hard hands smoothed over every inch of her body,

stroking and teasing her until she was too breathless and aroused to think.

Then, strong hands gripped her shoulders, turning her, and she opened her eyes to see Wreckage standing in front of her, smiling.

"Ready?" he asked.

"*Fraxx*, yes." She threw her arms around his neck and pulled him down so she could reach his mouth for a kiss. He dropped his head, his mouth mating with hers as he lifted her into the air.

She wrapped her legs around his hips, trapping his cock between them, the hard bar pressed against the seam of her pussy, so close to where she needed him to be.

Ruin moved, and she found herself sandwiched between her two lovers once again. His hands landed on her ass, parting her cheeks just a little so he could fit the hard shaft of his cock between them. The unexpected contact made her gasp, first in surprise and then delight.

Ruin blazed a trail of open-mouthed kisses down the side of her neck to her shoulder while Wreckage plundered her mouth with his, their tongues dancing. She caught hold of his shoulders, letting her nails bite into his skin as they lifted her together, two sets of hands positioning her to take Wreckage's cock.

"You're cheating and doing the silent talking thing." Not that she was complaining when everything they did felt so good.

Wreckage managed to slide a hand between them to play with her breasts as he eased himself into her channel. She willed herself to relax and enjoy as her body slowly gave way to his.

"Does he feel good inside you?" Ruin asked, the words muffled against her skin.

"Yes. So good. And I like what you're doing, too." Her words came out dreamy and soft.

Ruin rocked his hips, sliding his cock between her cheeks. "I like it, too. One of these days I'll fuck your ass while Wreck fucks your sweet pussy. Would you like that?"

She nodded mutely, too overwhelmed to speak. It was all so much, and she'd never expected Ruin to be a dirty talker. It was like they'd seen her darkest fantasies and were bringing them to life.

"Do you think you're the only one who dreamed about this moment?" Wreckage asked. "You weren't. We have plans for you, little goddess. All you have to do is let go."

She closed her eyes and let herself fall into a world of perfect pleasure, where every touch sent her senses spinning. Hard kisses, soft caresses, the flow of water gliding over skin. They fucked her together, hips rocking, strong hands holding her up as they claimed her one stroke at a time.

Ruin used soapy fingers to keep her slick for his cock as Wreckage drove himself deep inside, hitting nerves she'd never known she had.

She braced herself between them, arching her hips and twisting to get as much contact with them both as possible.

The thick head of Ruin's cock rubbed against her back hole, and something inside her broke, sending her spiraling into an orgasm so intense she could do nothing but ride out the storm raging inside her. Her cries echoed off the tile walls, a countermelody to the rhythmic slap of bodies coming together.

When Wreckage came, he grunted her name and thrust himself into her still-quivering channel, painting it with his cum.

A moment later, Ruin stiffened and jerked behind her, his teeth closing on her shoulder in a love bite that bordered on pain without crossing over.

"Oh, sweetling," Wreckage whispered against her mouth a few seconds later. "That was worth waiting for."

"Mhmm," she murmured in wordless agreement.

"Perfection. That's what you are." Ruin kissed the spot he'd just bitten and gently eased himself apart from her. "And when we get you in bed, we're going to do that again but better."

"Better than perfection?" She turned her head to smile at him. "I don't think that's possible."

"Then we'll die trying." Wreckage kissed her cheek tenderly.

Jade snickered.

"What's so funny?"

"I finally understand what Maggie meant when she told me the only thing that would save me were my medi-bots."

"She was right about that." Ruin caught her and slung her over his shoulder. "Ready for round two?"

Jade didn't know if she was ready or not, but she couldn't wait to do it anyway.

9

———

Ruin had decided that hover-bike was the best method of transport ever invented. Not only did it not require roads or speed limits, but it gave Jade a reason to be snuggled up right behind him, her hands locked around his waist. At least, that's where they stayed most of the time.

In the days and nights since she'd first visited the cabin, they'd discovered that their little goddess wanted them as much as they wanted her. And she wasn't afraid to make the first move.

He set them down in a clearing they hadn't visited before. Wildflowers covered the entire area, painting the space in a myriad of colors.

Once they were off the bike, Jade yanked off her helmet and tossed it to him. "This is amazing!" She ran out into the clearing, her hands brushing along the tops of the highest blooms.

He turned to set the helmet down on the bike, and by the time he turned around, Jade was gone.

Before he could call for her, she popped up from the field of flowers. Her face and outfit were streaked in pollen, and she had a bit of broken foliage in her hair. She raised her arms and threw back her head to stare up into the sky. "This is freedom, Ru. Glorious, beautiful freedom."

"Yes, it is," he agreed. But it wasn't the flowers that made him feel that way. It was seeing her abandon all decorum to romp in a field of flowers just because she felt like it. For him, any talk of freedom would always remind him of this moment... and her.

She picked several of the blooms and tucked them behind her ear before returning to his side. She smelled of the meadow, of warm grass, spring flowers, and something that was uniquely her. "Where are we going?"

"To a place I found when I was on patrol last week. I think you'll like it."

She took his hand and looked up at him with a joy-filled and trusting expression that made his chest tighten with sudden emotion. "If you're there and I'm there, I'm sure it will be perfect."

"This way," he managed to get the words out past a weird lump in his throat.

As they walked through the forest, he acted as a guide, showing her game trails and explaining what animals would use them. Rock claws' routes were the easiest to spot because the creatures tended to crash through the underbrush, leaving crushed plants and destruction in their wake.

"I had no idea they were so big," Jade stretched out her arms to span the meter-wide track. "I haven't seen one yet. I just know they're tasty."

Ruin slowed to look at her in surprise. "You haven't seen a rock claw?"

"Nope. By the time I was strong enough to leave the colony, they'd all gone into hibernation for the winter. Now they're back, but I've never come across one."

"There's one about three hundred meters up this path. I'll show you, but you have to stay behind me. They're slow, but their claws are strong enough to crush anything they clamp down on."

"Got it. I'll stay behind you. I like my limbs attached to my body." She went quiet for a few seconds, staring toward where he'd told her the rock claw was. "How do you know one is there?"

"Cyborg senses. I can hear it." It was one of the reasons he enjoyed the forest. Out here, he didn't need to dial down his senses to protect him from the sensory noise that bombarded him when he was in Haven.

The rock claw didn't pay them any attention as they approached, which was typical. The lumbering creatures were too well-armored to be bothered by most of the local predators, and they still hadn't learned that the newly arrived colonists were a threat they should avoid. Still, he had his kes'tarv in his hand, the metal rod fully extended in case the beast decided to be difficult.

"Oh! I get it now. They're big, but their leg span is what makes the trail so wide." Jade looked out from behind him but didn't move any farther. "Those claws are... *veth*. They could do real damage with those."

"They can, and they do. But there's an easy way to deal with them. Watch."

He walked up to the crab-like creature with his *kes'tarv* extended. The rock claw raised its claws in warning, snapping the massive limbs several times in quick succession.

Ruin ignored the warning. He stepped to the side and angled the staff in his hands between two of the animal's many legs. Then he pushed it over. It teetered and staggered in the direction he'd shoved it.

"And if pushing it doesn't work, you can do this." He extended the staff again, this time wedging it beneath the rock claw before bringing the *kes'tarv* up quickly. The motion sent the animal into the air, and it settled on its back.

Ruin stepped away. "They're vulnerable when they're upside down, but they don't usually stay that way for long. If you have to flip one, either kill it quickly or leave the area."

"Flip and run. Got it." She fell in beside him as they left the rock claw struggling to right itself. "Does this mean I get to carry one of those kes'tarv things you and Wreck carry?"

"I'll order one for you later today. Once it's made, Wreck and I will teach you how to use it." He never intended for Jade to go anywhere dangerous without one or both of them accompanying her, but she should still be prepared to defend herself if necessary.

"I'd like that. I'm already a decent scrapper and I'm not bad with a knife, but the kes'tarv is an elegant weapon. Plus, it's long enough I can put more distance between me and an attacker."

He hated that Jade's life had been so harsh that she'd needed to learn how to fight. Knife fighting was vicious and bloody, requiring the combatants to be in close quarters. Thus it forced them to experience each other's pain and potential deaths every second of the conflict. "I didn't know you could fight with a blade."

She shivered despite the warmth of the day. "I don't like to talk about it. I haven't carried a knife since I got to Haven. I hope I never need to carry one again."

He led her to their destination, pausing at the clearing's edge to scan it for any indication of danger. When he was satisfied, he glanced down at her and nodded. "Is it safe? Tell me what you see."

"I see a beautiful spot with sun-dappled shade, a lovely little brook, and plenty of soft grass and flowers to stretch out in. As for how safe it is, there's no blood vine I can see. The local wildlife is singing and buzzing, so there don't appear to be any predators about, and I can't see any rock claw tracks. I'm assuming that bark spiders have that name because they camouflage themselves to look like tree bark, so we shouldn't find any hidden among the flowers." She bounced on her toes. "So? How did I do?"

"Well enough. You missed the rock claw trail over there, but it's old and partially overgrown, so it's unlikely it's still in use." He leaned down to kiss her hair. "And you're right. Bark spiders are ambush predators. They like to drop onto their victims. They lack the ability to jump, so being on the ground puts them at a disadvantage."

Then he pointed across the little clearing to a large tree. "There's one on the trunk of that one, though. You won't be able to see it from this distance, but I can."

"So, it's not safe." She looked at him expectantly. "Not until you deal with the bark beastie. I will tackle a rock claw if I have to, but I'd rather leave the venomous creepy-crawly things to you or Wreck."

"Good policy."

He pulled out his *kes'tarv* and flicked the switch to extend it. He spun it in his hand as he strode over to the bark spider and then flicked the creature off the tree with the tip of the staff. He didn't give it a chance to escape. The moment it hit the ground, he stomped on it several times with his heavy boots.

"Now it's safe," he announced.

"Now it's squished!" Jade looked at him with amusement. "Subtle."

He retracted his staff and tucked it back into his belt before shrugging off the pack he carried. "Subtle is usually slow, and I have better things to do today."

"I can't argue with that."

He'd packed all the basics for a simple lunch, and the two of them soon had the blanket set out with packets of sandwiches, fruit slices, and canteens of water.

Jade sat with her legs crossed. He planned to sit across from her, but she caught his hand and pulled him toward her. Somehow, he ended up lying on his back with his head cradled in her lap.

"This is your day off, too. Relax, Ru. It's my turn to take care of you."

"I *am* relaxed."

She placed her hands on his brow and began to massage his temples. "Not yet, you're not."

Her soft hands and gentle touches *were* soothing, and after a few minutes, his breathing slowed and deepened. Her fingers drifted down to work on the hinge of his jaw and then up to his temples again.

"Better?" she asked, her voice soft and content.

"Better."

When she worked her way higher to massage his scalp, he actually groaned. It felt so good. It wasn't just her touch, either. It was the sense of connection he felt. It was intimate in a way he'd never experienced, just the two of them sharing a moment he'd never forget.

After a time, Jade spoke. "Ru? You still awake?"

He opened his eyes and smiled. "Of course. But one night I hope you'll do this for me again. I think it would help me sleep."

"Dreams?" she asked, her voice barely a whisper now.

"Nightmares," he confirmed.

"Me too. But they're better when I stay with you and Wreckage."

"Then stay with us more often." He hadn't intended to say that, but now the words were out. He had no regrets.

Jade shook her head. "I'm there most nights already, and neither of you has a bed big enough for the three of us. I heard Wreckage bitching when he smacked his head against the wall the other night."

"We've got a plan for that. We're going to knock out the wall between our rooms. We can extend the outer wall to give us a dressing room and a second bathroom. And before you say anything, we already planned for another bathroom. This isn't a big change."

"But it would be a lot of work," she protested. "I mean, extra work. There's just the two of you, and you have duties as rangers, too. I don't know much, but could I help somehow?"

Ruin laid his hand over hers. "We'll find something for you to do. I think you should leave the tree felling and heavy work to us, though."

She ran her hands through his hair and grinned. "How about I supervise that part? You two work shirtless and I'll watch and, uh, ensure you both stay fed and hydrated."

"Shirtless, huh? You have yourself a deal. And yes, I'm committing Wreck to this plan. Though he might want you to agree to the same conditions."

"You want me topless?"

"*Fraxx*, yes." He'd suggest she go entirely naked, but that wouldn't be smart while using axes and power tools.

"Agreed." She bent over, kissed him on the tip of his nose, and then went back to massaging his scalp. He let himself enjoy the moment. If he could entice her to move out to their cabin, it would make things easier for all of them.

Jade hadn't expected to love the woods as much as she did. The wild places and fresh air were a balm to her soul, healing wounds she didn't know she had. After a lifetime of living inside the sealed walls of a hive city, something was almost magical about being out in nature, surrounded by living things.

Being out here helped her understand why Ruin and Wreckage chose to live outside the colony. She could see herself out here, too. Not right away, but someday, after they'd been together long enough to be sure it was the right choice.

They lounged in comfortable silence for a time.

She tried to stay in the moment, but her thoughts kept drifting to things she didn't want to think about right now.

Eventually, Jade realized it would be easier to let them go if she told someone about her concerns. "I know this is a date, but I've got something on my mind, and I think I need to talk it through and get some advice."

Ruin opened one eye, his look one of mild concern. "Is this a feelings thing?"

She snickered. How could a man be fine with facing off against a massive land crab or stomping a venomous predator, but get squeamish over feelings? Men were *weird*. "Relax, Ru. It's a work thing."

"Then by all means, talk me through it."

"There's an anomaly in the colony's datasphere. It's minor and I've only seen it a few times, but every time I try to pin down exactly what it is, it vanishes."

"How would data vanish?" Ruin asked.

"It's not data, exactly. It's more like a presence that shouldn't be there." She pointed to the stream not far away. "If I threw a rock into the water, you'd see ripples. But you'd know the rock caused them to happen. I'm seeing a kind of ripple in cyberspace, but I can't see what caused it."

His dark brows scrunched as he considered what she'd said. "You've got a ghost."

"Yeah. I do. And it's smart enough to react every time I try to get a look at it. A random bit of rogue code could cause the ripple, but it couldn't react the way this ghost does." She shrugged, already feeling her shoulders tightening in frustration. "It might be nothing, but..."

"But your gut is telling you it might be *something*."

"Exactly."

"What do your teammates think it is? What did Phaedra say when you told her?"

The tension in her shoulders increased. "I haven't mentioned it to the others. And I'm not supposed to mention this, but Phaedra isn't available at the moment."

Ruin's eyes snapped open. "Not available?"

"Official word is the new doctor put her on bedrest and ordered her to relax as much as possible."

Ruin snorted. "I'm sure that went well. The princess has more untapped energy than a plasma storm. I can't see her being told to stay in bed and not do anything."

"Me either," Jade agreed. "But honestly, I don't think that's the whole story. I think their announcement about the baby has upset some beings. She figured that might happen. It's one of the reasons she recruited me. She mentioned having to go into hiding if things got bad." She sighed. "I'm afraid that's what really happened. They've secreted her away until things settle down."

"You think someone from the colony is a threat to Phaedra and her baby?" Ruin looked disturbed and uneasy. She knew how he felt. The idea of someone they knew doing something to an innocent child was chilling.

"I hope not. The news will have spread through the Vardarian empire by now. Maybe the *Liq'za* have reacted badly. Maybe the empress shed her scales when she heard the news. She's still not thrilled her brother left the empire to start his own colony."

"The *Liq'za*... Those are the Vardarians who want traditional values and racial purity. Right?"

"Yeah. I'm still surprised a race so advanced can be that messed up. I mean humans, sure. We're a shipwreck in progress. But I always assumed the other races had figured this stuff out."

"Not so, as you've noticed, with the possible exception of the Torskis. I've never met one that wasn't decent, kind, and generous."

"I've only met Denz, and he's half human," Jade admitted. "But I know Shadow adores his family. And Kade's fathers. It's just the mother none of them seem to talk about."

"That's because she did some vile things to her son and to her *mahoyen*. From what you've told me, she's probably one of those *Liq'za*, or at least moves in their circles. She's never accepted the fact Kade's fathers are in love with each other as well as with her."

"Which explains why they're in orbit around Liberty running their new shipyard, and Kade's mother has never visited. Shadow mentioned that, and I wondered how a Vardarian trio could manage to be apart so long."

"From what I've heard, it's better for everyone that they stay apart. But we got off track. I can understand why Phaedra would need to stay out of sight for a time, but why has she cut contact with you and the rest of her team?"

"That is probably my fault." Jade sighed before continuing, "After the announcement I noticed that my teammate, Allax, didn't look at all happy. I mentioned it to Phaedra, and she said she'd let Yardan know to keep an eye on him. I don't think he'd do anything to hurt Phaedra and I'm probably misreading the situation, but I bet she decided not to let any of us know where she was."

"Or her *mahoyen* made that decision for her," Ruin said.

"Or that."

"That's why you haven't spoken to the rest of your team about this?"

"Yes. Plus, it's not like they can see it. None of them are jacked in. They're skimmers. Good ones, but they can't do a deep dive like I can, and I'm limited, too."

"Then don't mention it to them. If one of them is in on it, you'd be putting yourself at risk. The palace may be safe for you, but the datasphere isn't. Not if someone on your team turns on you." He gave her an intent look. "Do *not* tell them, Jade."

She appreciated his concern, but she'd never been good at taking orders from anyone. Instead of agreeing not to tell anyone, she shifted the topic.

"If I had the full use of my remaining implants, I should be able to figure out what's going on." Without thinking about it, she raised one hand to rub her sole remaining data port behind her ear.

"You want to be at your full potential. I can understand that. But the risks…"

"I know. I don't want to die, but this is what I'm *good* at. Thanks to the setup Phaedra put together for me, I'm decent again, but I miss being really good at it. Those bastards didn't just rip out my implants. They tore away part of who I was, and I want it back."

Ruin sat up suddenly and then caught her in his arms and pulled her onto his lap. "I understand. I don't want you to do it, but that's because I don't want to lose you." He growled like a disgruntled beast and buried his face into her hair. "But that's not my choice to make. I believe you're smart and capable enough to do your job without trying to reactivate your remaining implants."

"Thank you for believing in me." She meant every word. For years, the only one to have faith in her abilities was Maggie. His support was a gift, one that made her feel guilty she was even considering the surgery.

"Always, little goddess."

"I got a message from the new doctor yesterday.

She's reached out to all the humans currently in the colony to see if we'd like to have a preliminary appointment with her. I think I need to talk to her and see if this is something she can help me with."

Ruin didn't move except to tighten his hold. "And if she says yes?"

"I don't know. I just want to know what my options are."

Silence.

Just as she was about to say something to break the tension, Ruin raised his head and sighed. "You tricked me. You said we weren't going to talk about feelings. I think you should be punished for that."

A wave of anticipation ran through her, pushing all serious thoughts aside. "Will this involve orgasms?"

"Several."

She shivered at the lust in his voice. "Are you sure this is really a punishment?"

He dropped his head to her ear and whispered, "Who said the orgasms would all be yours?"

10

———

WANDERING through the colony with Jade was rapidly becoming one of Wreckage's favorite things to do. Before this, he'd always arrived with a list of items they needed and a plan to get it all done as efficiently as possible.

With Jade, it was different. They'd pick directions at random, exploring areas of the ever-expanding colony. She chatted with shopkeepers, which he discovered was a great way to find new places to eat and other shops to visit.

She was more social and outgoing than he had ever been, and it paid off in ways he'd never considered. It made him question yet again the choice Ruin and he had made to isolate themselves. They were missing out on more than they'd realized, all because of a secret he was tired of keeping.

"You're quiet today," Jade said.

"I'm not as good at socializing as you are. You make it look easy."

Jade made a dismissive flicking gesture with one hand and laughed. "A waitress who doesn't talk and make their customers feel at ease usually doesn't have a job for long. Do it long enough, and it becomes second nature.

"Though I have to admit, I'm happy I don't *need* to do that anymore. My new job doesn't require small talk and banter. Now, if I want to talk, I can. If I want to go for a walk in the woods and enjoy the silence? I can do that, too."

"How do you feel about walking in the rain?" He glanced upward to draw her attention to the dark clouds crowding out the sun. "Because I think that's about to happen."

"Rain is best enjoyed indoors. Otherwise, it's a bit like taking a stroll through a cold shower you can't turn off." She looked at the sky and wrinkled her nose. "We're going to get wet, and not in the fun way."

"Not necessarily. We can make it to your place if you let me drive."

"Drive?" she asked, confused. "We walked here."

"But you have the option of using the cyborg express delivery service." He opened his arms and grinned. "All aboard."

She squealed with delight and stepped close

enough for him to sweep her into his arms. "Home, please."

"You got it, sweetling."

He took off at close to his full speed, fast enough to get them home before the rain while still allowing for enough reaction time to avoid pedestrians and other obstacles.

Jade whooped and laughed as they raced the weather. "This is almost as good as a hover-bike ride!"

"Glad you're enjoying it."

He didn't slow until they reached the bridge. The crowds were thicker here, and he had less room to maneuver.

Jade took it all in stride, waving to beings she knew and calling out warnings to finish their errands and get inside before the weather turned.

The first drops of rain pattered down as he reached the stairs leading up to her apartment. He put on one final burst of speed and lengthened his stride to take the steps two at a time.

They tumbled through the door together, both laughing as the downpour started in earnest.

"Nicely done." Jade shook a few stray raindrops from her hair and walked over to the window. "Shall we watch everyone run for cover?"

He joined her, choosing to stand behind her with one arm hooked around her waist to draw her in close.

From here they could watch as some shoppers

hurried off to find shelter while others seemed to ignore the rain completely. Vendors shuffled their inventory to get some items under cover while looking out with a mixture of annoyance and resignation.

The rain came down harder until the view was blurred by the water flowing down the glass. Then, he got an idea.

Wreckage swept her hair back, exposing the long line of her throat. He nibbled at her ear lobe, waiting until she tipped her head to one side in invitation to continue.

He moved along the column of her neck, kissing her softly. She leaned against him, her ass grinding gently against his rapidly hardening cock.

Without warning, he slid his hands under her shirt to cup her breasts.

"Ack! Cold hands," she yelped but didn't push him away.

He felt the skin beneath his lips heat as her arousal increased despite her complaint.

"Cold hands, hot sex. Isn't that the saying?"

"Not even close. Is that the best line you could come up with?"

"Take it as a compliment. It's hard to think when I'm touching you like this."

"Mmm. That was much better." She turned her head, putting her lips enticingly close to his. He leaned in and kissed her, capturing her moans as she rocked and writhed against him.

His fingers toyed with the hard peaks of her nipples as they teased each other, the friction between them growing hotter by the second.

"Bend over. Hands on the windowsill."

She obeyed, and he slid his hands out from under her shirt. He reached around her to unfasten her pants, sliding them down her hips before dropping to his knees to finish undressing her. Shoes. Socks. Pants. Panties, he stripped them from her one item at a time.

"Do you think anyone will see us up here?" He heard a note of longing in her voice and recalled her comment about not caring who saw them kissing her.

"Do you want them to see us?"

She swallowed and then glanced over her shoulder to meet his eyes. "I want them to know what we're doing, but they don't have to see everything. Does that make sense?"

He understood what she wanted. "It does. But there are rules. No one gets to see you naked but Ruin or me. That means your shirt stays on."

Jade nodded, her next breath coming out in a rush. She smiled as she moved her head to stare out at the water-blurred view.

Once she was naked from the waist down, he guided her legs farther apart and then eased himself between them. With his back to the wall and his legs stretched out on the floor, his mouth was almost perfectly aligned with her sex.

"*Fraxx* me. Are you going to—" her question

morphed into a low, needy moan as he parted her labia with his fingers and ran his tongue across the slick flesh of her pussy.

Her reaction was everything he wanted. She bucked against his face, soft cries of pleasure falling from her lips as he licked and lapped at her core.

Her cream covered his mouth and chin, scenting the air with her arousal as he focused his attention on her clit.

Within minutes she was panting and breathless, her trembling legs telling him just how close she was to orgasm. Then, and only then, did he slide two fingers into her wet heat, fucking her with them until she came.

He crawled out from between her legs and rose, his hands already tugging down his pants to free his aching cock.

"Don't move." He'd been in her home before and knew exactly what he needed to make this work. He crossed over to a padded footstool he'd used more than once on his visits and set it down at her feet.

"Stand on that, sweetling."

She obeyed him with an eagerness that made his cock twitch in anticipation. Their little goddess was always so strong and independent, but they'd discovered that when it came to sex, she was different. She trusted them to pleasure and protect her, allowing herself to soften when they were alone.

He moved in behind her, one arm looping around her waist to help her balance as he fisted his cock in his other hand. Their reflection in the window was blurry and indistinct, but it was enough for him to know that no one would be able to see her naked except for him.

Perfect.

He eased himself into place and then held still, the head of his cock pressed against the heat of her opening. She shivered and pushed back from the window, driving herself onto his shaft. He groaned and surged his hips forward, burying himself inside her.

Jade rose on her toes, her breathy moan fogging the window as their bodies joined. Her inner walls flexed around him, squeezing his cock and sending a jolt of raw pleasure straight to his balls. He reached out to wrap the dark strands of her hair around his fist, pulling her head back as he withdrew and then drove into her again.

The little sounds she made nearly broke his control, but he would not let it end this fast. He wanted to give Jade everything she wanted, and that included an audience.

He took her hard and fast until their world was reduced to tiny details that flashed by in a torrent of ecstasy—the slap of skin on skin, the uneven rhythm of his breath, the way her cries rose in volume. When he'd taken them both to the brink, he leaned over and whispered in her ear. "If you want everyone to know what we're doing, all you have to do is scream, sweetling. Scream my name when you come, and they'll all hear you."

She moaned and twisted her head to look at him. The motion pulled her hair out of his grasp, freeing his hand at the perfect moment.

"Give me a reason, and I'll do the rest," she said, her voice half wild with need.

He'd never been with anyone who made him feel like this. Sex with Jade was so much more than the act of fucking. She was his match in every way.

Holding on to that thought, he slapped her ass with just enough force to sting and then reached around to delve between her legs and find her swollen clit. He pressed down, and she broke like a wave on a rocky shore. Her cries filled his ears as her entire body stiffened, milking his cock and breaking the last threads of his control.

"You tell them," he growled. "Tell them who you belong to."

"Yes, Wreck. Yes!"

He came hard, groaning her name as he spent himself inside her. Each time one of them moved, the other one responded with another moan or tremor that prolonged the moment. "You are mine, sweetling. And now they all know it."

As if to confirm his words, loud cheers and more than a few catcalls erupted from the tavern below her apartment.

"*Veth.* I had no idea so many people were downstairs."

He withdrew from her gently and then lifted her off the footstool and away from the window. "It's raining out there. Where did you think everyone went to escape the downpour?"

She threw her arms around him, laughing as she kissed him. "You don't have to sound quite so smug about it."

"Hell yes I do. Now they all know Ruin and I have the hottest, sexiest woman on the planet, and they'll just have to settle for second best." He wrapped her in his arms and held her tightly, reveling in the moment.

They stayed that way until a chime announced something was being sent up from the tavern's kitchen. Jade buried her face against his chest and cursed. "Saral must be working today. I can't imagine what she thought to send us. Can you check? I don't want to die of embarrassment.

He ambled over to the dumbwaiter that had been installed when the tavern was built. Inside was a tray with a single serving of their signature dessert, "Almost Heaven," with two spoons. He burst out laughing, recalling the first time he'd tasted the dish. It was the night Striker had taken out Thrash for daring to touch Maggie and then carried her out of the tavern over his shoulder.

"What is it?" Jade asked.

"My favorite dessert and two spoons."

"That's... almost tame for her. You sure that's all there is?"

He looked again, this time spotting a note written on a napkin. "There's a note. It says, *Three orgasms are better than two. You're not done yet.*"

Jade groaned and buried her face in her hands. "I'm never going to be able to look that female in the face again."

"She just wants what's best for you." He leered at her. "And she has a point. First, we eat. Then we shower. Somewhere between those, we'll go for three orgasms."

"We don't have time for all of that. My appointment with Dr. Clark is in an hour." Neither of them had mentioned the appointment until now. She was anxious about it, and he hadn't wanted to ruin their date by mentioning it when she was clearly trying to avoid thinking about it.

"You won't be late. After all, you can always request another cyborg express delivery."

Her smile lit up the room and made his heart swell. "You'd take me to the appointment?"

"Of course. I can wait for you outside if you like, too."

She shook her head, and for a moment he thought she was about to tell him she didn't want him to do that, that she wasn't ready for him to be involved. "You don't have to wait outside, Wreck. If you like, you can come in with me. It would be nice to have someone in my corner."

"Anything you need from me, sweetling. All you have to do is ask." The words were easy to say, but he meant what he said. Whatever she needed. Whatever she wanted. He'd find a way to give it to her.

11

———

THEY ENDED up walking to her appointment with no need for an express delivery. Now they were outside the med-center, but Jade wasn't sure she wanted to go in.

Wreckage seemed to sense her hesitation. He stayed close, using his big body to block the chill breeze flowing past them. The rain had eased off to a constant drizzle so light it was more mist than rain. She huddled deeper into her jacket and tried to work out where her doubts came from.

It didn't take long to work it out. Until now, this decision hadn't affected anyone else. She and Maggie had long since made peace with the risks they both took in their fight to survive and eventually escape Earth.

Falling for Wreckage and Ruin had changed that. It changed *everything*. She couldn't say when it had happened, but she couldn't deny her feelings, even if she wasn't ready to admit to them yet. They'd given her everything she'd dreamed of and more. Was it selfish of her to want this? To risk this new life just to have part of her old one back?

A rowdy group of males, both cyborg and Vardarian, spilled out the door of an eatery and into the street. The noise startled her, and the sudden arrival of so many loud males sent her into a panic.

She turned and pressed herself against Wreckage. Hiding her face against his chest and locking her shaking hands tightly around his waist.

He wrapped her in his arms, bowing his head over hers. "I got you, sweetling."

Her throat tightened to the point she couldn't speak, but she gave him an extra hard squeeze to convey her gratitude. This was so *fraxxing* embarrassing. She thought she had this all under control, and now here she was, having a minor meltdown in front of everyone. In front of Wreckage.

"Take a deep breath," he told her. "I know it sounds stupid, but do it anyway."

She tried, but she felt like a steel band was wrapped around her chest and all she could manage was a shallow sip of air.

"No? Okay. New plan." He caught her chin in one hand and firmly raised her head so she had to look at him.

Then he kissed her.

It was the sweetest kiss she'd ever had. His lips were soft and coaxing, his blue eyes never leaving hers. She exhaled the air that had been locked in her lungs and he hummed in approval.

He kissed her again, his fingers stroking her cheek as she managed to take one normal breath and then another. He kept it up until her hands stopped shaking and her mind functioned properly.

"Thank you. I... that..." She leaned away from him and gestured to herself. "I hate that it still happens. It's so stupid."

"Nuh-uh. It's not stupid. It's just biological wiring. There's not a cyborg on this planet who hasn't gone through what just happened to you, including me."

"I've never seen you lock up like that." Wreckage and Ruin always seemed unshakable, too strong to be bothered by anything as petty as fear.

"Because my triggers aren't the same as yours, and I've had more time to deal with what happened to me. It gets easier over time."

"That's what they keep telling me. What I hear is that this is never going to stop."

"You'll learn to get ahead of it. It just takes time and practice." He smiled down at her. "Trust me on that one."

"I do trust you. I'm curious, though. How did you know kissing me would work?"

"I didn't. But it was easier than trying to walk you through a grounding exercise." His grin widened. "You know. Name three things you can see, hear, and smell."

She laughed, and the last of her tension melted away. "I've done that. Your way works a lot better."

"It was more fun, too. Next time you feel that way, you have my permission to jump in my arms and kiss me. I'm sure Ruin will love the plan."

"No doubt about it." She stepped out of his embrace and gave herself a quick mental shake. "Let's get inside before anything else happens."

And before she changed her mind about seeing this new doctor to discuss her options.

It turned out that the doctor had brought a medic with her, and the two of them worked together like two halves of a whole. Dr. Jody Clark had salt and pepper hair, kind eyes, and a smile that immediately put Jade at ease. Loris, the medic, was a gray-haired woman with a soft voice and gentle smile.

"I'm so glad you came in to see us," Dr. Clark said once they'd introduced themselves and moved to one of the examination rooms. "I've looked over your file and the notes Dr. Li left. Before we talk about future plans, I'd like to know how you're doing at the moment."

"I'm fine." It was the same response she gave to almost everyone.

"No, she's not," Wreckage stated and shot her a

knowing look. "She had a panic attack outside just before we came in."

Feeling betrayed, Jade tried to tug her hand free from Wreckage's grip, but he didn't allow it.

"Lying about it doesn't change what happened," he said, his voice soft but firm. "Dr. Clark needs to know."

The fact he was right didn't help much, but she stopped trying to pull away. "Okay, I'm mostly fine. Good appetite, getting enough sleep, started a new job, too." She raised the hand still clasped in Wreckage's. "And I'm dating, as you may have noticed."

Dr. Clark smiled and nodded. "So I see. That's all good to hear. And it's obvious he's watching out for you."

"*We* are," Wreckage said.

The doctor nodded but didn't otherwise react to this announcement. "I'm glad to hear it. If you decide to go through with the procedure, having a supportive team around you will speed up your recovery."

"We'll take care of her," Wreckage said.

Despite her earlier annoyance, she couldn't help but smile and squeeze Wreckage's fingers. He had been doing what was best for her, even when she didn't want him to. And he was here, ready to support her decision no matter what.

"Now, about the incident outside. Do you know what triggered it?" the doctor asked.

Jade explained what had happened. She knew

what her triggers were. She just hadn't figured out how to stop the response before it overpowered her.

The doctor listened and made a few notes. Once Jade was done, she asked a few follow-up questions and then smiled.

"I know it doesn't feel like it sometimes, but you are progressing well. You're already aware of what causes the reaction and you can regain control quite quickly, especially if you have a little help. You will find your way through this, Jade. I am certain of it."

"Thanks. I just want this to be over and done with. But I'll be patient if I have to."

Loris chuckled softly. "Spoken like every cyber-jock I've ever met."

That caught Jade's attention. "You say that like you've met a lot of us."

"I have. This isn't my first career. Back in the day, most of my clients were cyber-jockeys looking for implants and upgrades."

She stared at the older woman in shock. If that was the case, her chances of regaining her abilities had improved by light years. "You were an installer? Where?"

"Here and there. I even worked out in the Drift for a time. Ran into some trouble eventually and decided it was time to try something legit before I got myself killed." She opened her hands. "And here I am. I've been with Jody here for more than ten years. This opportunity was too perfect to pass up." She winked at the doctor. "And she'd be lost without me."

"Indeed I would, though I am impressed with Rae, the holographic program that manages the various med-centers here. I've never seen anything like it."

"She's amazing," Jade agreed. "And has a better bedside manner than some doctors I've met. Did you know they've just linked her to the med-bay on the orbital platform?"

"We did. It makes sense. That way there's always a med-tech, or in this case a healer of sorts, on the station in case of emergencies," Dr. Clark said.

"I love that she keeps immaculate records. Unlike someone I could mention," she said, her tone light and teasing.

The doctor laughed. "Guilty as charged. But we should get back to you, Jade. I've reviewed your file and put together a plan for returning your remaining implants to full functionality."

"Full?"

"Full," Dr. Clark confirmed.

"I've seen the reports and inventoried what will need repairs versus what needs replacement," Loris took over the conversation, her tone steady and confident. "I know it doesn't seem that way, but you were actually fortunate in some ways. The damage to your cranial implant is mostly external."

"Lucky? If you say so." Jade wasn't sure that word

applied to any part of what had been done to her. "What are the risks?"

Wreckage tensed beside her, waiting for their answer.

"I'm not going to sugar coat it. The risks are higher than I'd like." Dr. Clark folded her hands in her lap, her gaze steady. "We will take every precaution we can, but in the end, there's no way to test the connection without fully activating the implant."

"And once we do that, any hidden damage will likely malfunction," Jade finished. She'd heard this before. It was why she hadn't gone through with the procedure yet.

"I will do everything I can to ensure that doesn't happen. I'd like to do an exam and take more scans before you leave today. If that's alright?" Loris said.

"Please. The more information you have, the better my chances are. Right?" Jade tried to make the comment sound light and jokey, but she wasn't sure she managed it.

"What are the odds of something going wrong?" Wreckage asked.

Loris and Dr. Clark exchanged a look before the doctor spoke. "Jade, do you want to hear this? Some patients don't want to know exact numbers."

"I'm a cyber-jockey. Data is my life. I want to know." Only when she heard her own words did Jade realize what she'd said. I *am* a cyber-jockey. Not *was*. Even without this procedure, her new job had given her back her identity. Did that mean she shouldn't take the risk?

"There's an eighty-seven percent chance we can return your implant to full functionality with no issues. In that case, your recovery will take less than a day, thanks to your medi-bots."

"And the other thirteen percent?" Jade asked.

Dr. Clark pursed her lips and blew out a soft breath before she answered, "There's a two percent chance something goes wrong while you are anesthetized. That's a standard factor. The rest comes down to what happens when we activate your implant. If something goes wrong, there's no good outcome. You could suffer brain damage, permanent loss of the implant, or death."

"*Fraxx*," Wreckage muttered.

"Those are better odds than what Dr. Li gave me." She smiled at Loris. "You just upped my chances by a fair margin."

The older woman shot her a cocky grin that made her look far younger. "I'm good at what I do. And if I didn't think we could pull this off, I'd tell you so."

"We're not going to take chances with your life, Jade. We believe this is possible," Dr. Clark said.

"Do I need to give you an answer now?" she asked.

The doctor waved a hand in the negative. "Oh no. Think about it as long as you need to. We'll do the scans and update the records before you leave. After that, it's up to you. The procedure itself will take less than two hours, and then a few hours here at the med-center while you recover."

"And it's not like we're going to be run off our feet with patients for the foreseeable future," Loris said. "Fewer humans live on this planet than we normally see in a day."

"Which means you have time to settle in and get to know your new home. Speaking of which, you really need to check out a restaurant called Earthly Delights. The food is amazing, especially since they're recreating human dishes with local ingredients. Oh, and the cooks are both Vardarians."

"And if you haven't been to the Bar None yet, it's one of my favorites," Wreckage said. He still didn't look happy about what he'd learned, but he was trying to be pleasant.

"We were there yesterday." Loris patted her stomach. "I'm going to get fat living here. I've lived on space stations all my life. I've never seen so much fresh food."

"Or breathed air that's never seen the inside of a recycler," Jade said. "I know what you mean about the food, though. I've never eaten so well. In fact, we're headed to the Bar None after this to meet up with our third partner. We've got a lot to talk about."

After that, Wreckage left them to sit in the waiting room while they took more scans and did a thorough workup. Loris took note of what implants she had, who had installed them, and how long she'd had them. She also took scans of the areas where her implants had been torn out.

"They did a number on you. Didn't they?" Loris asked her gently as she looked at the scans.

"They did. But I'm still here and they're all dead, so…" she shrugged.

Loris lapsed into the coded language hackers used to communicate when they didn't want to be overheard. "You're a survivor. That's why I know this procedure is going to work." She winked. "But don't tell the doc I said that. She prefers I keep things professional."

"Lips sealed. Files locked. Thank you," Jade replied in the same language.

As Loris turned away, a thought occurred to Jade. In Galactic Standard she asked, "Did Phaedra ask you both to come here?"

Both women smiled, but Loris answered. "Who do you think installed that girl's first implants? Back then she was a pink-haired lunatic with big dreams and no filters. Now she's an alien *princess*."

"And she still has big dreams and no filters," Jade quipped. Thinking about Phaedra reminded her of her friend's current situation. She was in hiding to protect herself and her baby, but Dr. Clark would be in touch. She'd have to be, since Phaedra was her most important patient.

"If you happen to see her? Please tell her we miss her and I'd love it if she could message me."

Neither woman said anything, but Dr. Clark dropped her head slightly in acknowledgment. Then they went back to work.

By the time she left, Jade still didn't know if she would undergo the procedure or not. The first step would be to join Ruin for dinner so the three of them could talk about it. They were important to her, and she knew she needed to include them in this process. This wasn't just about her anymore, and they deserved for her to be as open and honest with them as they'd been with her.

Would it be worth risking what she had now to regain part of who she'd been? She couldn't answer that question yet. But she'd figure it out eventually. She had plenty of time.

12

Ruin already regretted agreeing to meet them at the tavern, and they hadn't even arrived yet.

The place was busier than usual, and for some reason, everyone kept looking his way and grinning. He had no idea what the joke was, but the level of attention made him twitchy, and he was already on edge. Jade hadn't had any luck figuring out what she'd seen in the system, and concern gnawed at him. Was it a glitch or something dangerous? If Jade pursued this on her own, would that make her a target? What if she decided to risk the procedure so she could track down this digital ghost?

He rolled his shoulders in an attempt to release some of the tension he felt. It failed, of course. That wouldn't happen until they were away from this place and he could talk to Jade.

"Where the fraxx are you?" he sent to Wreckage.

The sooner they arrived the sooner they could head upstairs and talk in private. He'd already put in their orders and the kitchen would send it upstairs when it was ready. If Wreckage didn't move his ass, the food would get there ahead of them.

"Cool your boosters. We're just outside. Coming through the door in three-two-one..."

Wreckage and Jade walked in—and were met by a rousing chorus of cheers and hoots from most of the patrons. *What the hell is that about?*

To make things worse, Wreckage didn't even try to keep a low profile. He raised both hands in the air like a prizefighter, grinning from ear to ear while Jade covered her eyes with one hand and laughed.

Ruin caught some of the comments as the two of them worked their way through the crowd to his table.

"Show off."

"Lucky bastards."

"When's the next shipment of female colonists supposed to arrive?"

He stood to meet them. Well, he stood for Jade. Wreckage didn't warrant that kind of treatment.

"How'd it go?" he asked as he pulled Jade in for a brief hug. He wanted to kiss her, but too much attention was directed their way already.

"Better than I hoped," she said.

"But there's still a thirteen percent chance something will go wrong," Wreckage sent to him.

Fraxx. That wasn't a number he was comfortable

with, but he couldn't say anything without revealing Wreckage's update. Jade never liked it when they communicated directly instead of aloud. Besides, this wasn't a topic for public consumption.

"Why don't we go upstairs for this conversation?" he said.

A second later, someone clapped him on the back. "*Conversation*. Right," Thrash drawled. His innuendo was about as subtle as a plasma grenade.

"Lucky bastards."

Ruin spun around to face Thrash, knocking the other cyborg's hand away as he moved. "Don't," he growled into Thrash's face.

Thrash's eyes went wide with surprise, but he didn't back down. "Don't what? It was a compliment."

"It was a sleazy comment and you know it, Thrash," Jade interjected. She stepped between the two of them and placed her hand on Ruin's chest while keeping her eyes on the idiot who needed to upgrade his verbal filters.

"Did it ever occur to you that this might be why you're single?" she asked.

"Are you saying I need better material?" Thrash asked.

"You need better manners," she retorted.

"You also need to apologize," Wreckage moved in behind Jade, clearly ready to move her out of harm's way if Thrash didn't back off.

The three of them glared at each other in stony

silence. The rest of the guests watched quietly, waiting to see what happened next.

Thrash swallowed and appeared to be about to say something when Jade frowned and lifted one hand. Her gaze bounced from Thrash to Wreckage and back to him several times as she used her hand to block out part of their faces. He realized what was happening too late to stop it.

"I never realized how similar you three look. Is there such a thing as batch-cousins?" she asked.

"No," his denial came out more like a guttural growl than anything resembling language.

"We don't look anything alike." Wreckage backed away, pulling Jade with him.

"Actually, you do," Blaze said from his seat not far away. "I didn't notice before."

"Must be that peach fuzz Thrash calls a beard," Talon called out to another round of laughter.

Thrash didn't react except to stare at Ruin, his hand rising to touch the beard he'd only recently started to grow.

"We all know we were created from DNA the asshole Grays stole from the Vault of the Fallen." Ruin shrugged as if this was nothing, but his heart slammed against his ribs and his brain screamed that this was it. Their secret was out.

"What corporation were you and Wreckage owned by? I can't remember you ever mentioning it," Thrash said.

"Torex. Not that it matters. You were created after the war. Me and Wreck were created during it. You know this."

Thrash jutted out his jaw. "It matters because I lost all my batch-siblings in that hell hole. If we're related somehow, I'd like to know."

"We're *not!*" Ruin roared. "Get the *fraxx* out of my face. Now. You can apologize to Jade later. We. Are. Leaving."

He turned and walked away, leaving Thrash alone. It was a calculated risk, but he didn't think Thrash would come after him. The other man was brash, but he wasn't stupid. If they fought, it would get ugly. Worse, Thrash would get banned from the tavern. Anya didn't tolerate violence inside her place.

A path cleared ahead of him as everyone stood aside or scooted their chairs out of his way. It wasn't like him to make a scene or draw attention, and he could hear the confused murmurings already starting behind him. Now they'd be the focus of even more attention. *Fraxxing* fantastic.

He caught up to Wreckage and Jade at the door. She was puzzled and unhappy. Wreckage's face was a blank mask, but he could see the regret and worry in his batch-brother's eyes.

The moment they were outside, Ruin caught Jade by the wrist and led her around to the alley and the stairs to her apartment.

Anger burned in his gut and adrenaline coursed

through his body, making him move faster than he realized.

"Stop," Jade said, but he ignored her. He had to get away from the tavern and everyone inside, especially Thrash. Of all the cyborgs at the bar, why did he have to be the one to come close enough for Jade to notice the similarities?

The *fraxxing* idiot might look more like him, but he'd inherited Wreckage's flair for the dramatic.

"Ow! Ruin. Stop. I can't keep up and you're hurting me."

Jade's distressed cry broke through his dark fog and he jerked to a halt. Awareness caught up to him a split second later. He'd been moving at cyborg speed, dragging Jade with him while Wreckage had done his best to help her keep up. He hadn't paid attention to his grip, either, and when he released Jade's wrist, she snatched her hand back and cradled it against her body like it hurt.

What had he done?

"Fraxx. I'm sorry. I didn't mean—"

She backed away from him, her gaze wary. "Doesn't matter what you meant. You did it. I want to know why. What the hell happened in there to make you so angry?"

Jade turned to look at Wreckage. "He's mad and you look like the world is about to end."

"We don't talk about it," Wreckage said.

Jade folded her arms and glowered. "Not good

enough. I've shared everything with the two of you. My fears, my scars, all of it. Why won't you do the same for me?"

Ruin clenched a hand into the hair at the back of his head and tried to clear his mind. "I'm sorry, Jade. You know I'm more comfortable away from crowded places. You have your triggers and I have mine. That's all it was."

Her expression hardened. "I don't think that's all it was. Thrash was an idiot, and I get that what he did would piss you off. That doesn't explain your reaction when I mentioned that you look similar enough to be related."

Wreckage put his hand on her shoulder. "This isn't the place to have a private conversation."

"We're not having a conversation about that. Period. We're here to talk about what happened at Jade's appointment and why a thirteen percent chance of something going wrong is too high to risk."

Jade bristled. "You two were talking behind my back again. Dammit, we discussed this! And thirteen percent is not too high. I was considering it when it was over twenty."

"Twenty?" Wreckage looked horrified. "Hell no."

Jade stared at them in silence, her arms folded and jaw tight. Silence hung over the three of them as the rain battered down and a chill that had nothing to do with the weather seeped into his reinforced bones.

"Why would you get a say when both of you are

hiding things from me? Secrets and relationships don't mix well." With a heavy sigh she uncrossed her arms and walked away from them, heading toward the stairs.

Ruin moved to follow her, but she threw out a hand without looking back. "No. I need to be alone right now. I think we've said enough to each other already." Her voice cracked on the last word, and Ruin's heart twisted in his chest. He'd done this. First, he'd hurt her wrist, and then he'd done more harm with his stupid words.

Fraxx. Fraxx. Fraxx. It was all falling apart.

"Jade." Wreckage called to her. "We're sorry. Some of the things we've been through... we've never talked about them. You matter to us, sweetling."

She was halfway up the stairs by this point, but she slowed and twisted around to look at them. It might have just been the rain, but Ruin thought he saw tears on her cheeks as she gazed down at the two of them. "I know. And you matter to me, too, but this isn't going to work unless things change. Think about that. Okay?"

They stood and watched her walk away from them without saying a word. What was there to say? The day he'd feared had finally arrived, and it had done more damage than he'd imagined. Word of what happened today would spread quickly, and soon some of the other cyborgs would realize they also bore a resemblance to him and Wreckage. The truth would come out soon. Even if they found a way to apologize to Jade for today, he wasn't sure she'd forgive them once she knew the truth.

Thrash and some of the others didn't simply share a few traces of the same genes. For all intents and purposes, those cyborgs were their children. And they had failed to protect every single one of them.

Jade didn't go inside right away. She stood on her deck with her hands on the railing until she felt as cold and gray as the weather. From here she could see the river, and beyond it the woods where Ruin and Wreckage lived. This morning, she had been looking forward to her next visit. Now, she wasn't sure she'd ever see their place again.

She ran her fingers over the spot where Ruin had gripped her so tightly. The pain hadn't been what made her protest at the time. It was the way he'd dragged her along behind him. It felt too much like the way the mercenaries had treated her. This time, the flashback hadn't made her freeze, though. It made her angry.

Was that what it was like for Ruin? She thought it must be. It would explain why he'd reacted to Thrash the way he had. It didn't explain why neither of them would talk about the other issue, though. She'd opened her life and her heart to them. They hadn't done the same. It felt disrespectful somehow, as if she was giving more of herself than they were. What could they possibly have done that was so bad they never spoke of it?

Shivering and soaked to the skin, she eventually went inside. By the time she was warm and dry again, she'd made a decision. She would get the procedure done. She wouldn't worry about what her lovers wanted. Wreckage had told Ruin the odds before she could explain, and Ruin had made his feelings clear. Neither of them liked the odds. But it wasn't like the numbers would ever improve. Loris's unique experience as an installer gave Jade a real chance of regaining her abilities.

She wanted it back. All of it. She needed to be at her best so she could track down the digital ghost in the system and identify it. If it was just a bug, fine. If it was a threat to her home or her friends, she had to stop it before someone got hurt. No one else could do what she could.

The only question left was who she'd tell beforehand. The answer was easy. She only wanted to talk to one person right now—Maggie. Everyone else would have to wait. Decision made, she tapped her comm unit and called up Dr. Clark's contact details.

A brief flash of doubt struck as she made the call, but she squelched it fast. "Sorry, guys. If you're going to keep secrets, so am I."

An hour later, it was all arranged. She'd leave work an hour early and go directly to the med-center. If all went well, she'd be back at work the next morning after spending the night under medical supervision.

If it didn't, Maggie had several messages to deliver, explaining her decision and saying goodbye.

"You better not die, Jaybird. If you do, I will have to hunt you down and smack you around in the afterlife." Maggie sat on a chair in Jade's living room with an unhappy expression on her face.

"I don't plan on dying. I just need to plan for all possible outcomes. You know that's how I'm wired."

"I know. That doesn't mean I have to like it." Maggie's eyes narrowed over her cup of tea. "I need to ask you something."

"Of course you do." Jade already suspected what her friend wanted to know.

"Are you doing this because you want to find this ghost? Or is it because you're mad at Wreckage and Ruin?"

"I need to do more, Magpie. And this new doctor has a medic with lots of experience with implants like mine. If anyone can make this work, it's Jody and Loris."

"Uh huh." Maggie didn't sound convinced. "Remember who you're talking to."

Jade huffed out a soft laugh. "Fine. It's ninety-five percent about doing my job and getting my life back, and five percent snark."

Maggie raised one brow and said nothing.

"Okay," Jade relented. "It's more like ten percent snark. But I'm not going to risk my life just to get back at my guys."

"Good to hear. I figured as much, but I wanted to be sure you weren't lying to yourself. This is a big deal."

"I know. But it's the right thing for me to do." The more she thought about it, the more convinced she was that she needed to do it. She'd even sent a message to Yardan, the grumpy spymaster, telling him about the digital ghost and why she was worried about it. Her gut instinct said this was a real threat.

"I got that. You wouldn't have told Yardan if you weren't legitimately worried."

"*Fraxx* no. He might have mellowed some, but he's still overly suspicious and distrustful. I guess it comes with the job. But now he knows everything I do. Truth be told, I should have told him sooner."

"Given the way he behaved in the past, I don't blame you." Maggie still hadn't forgiven the spymaster for the way he'd dealt with the Helix Fever crisis last winter. His xenophobic paranoia had almost cost the colony dearly, and none of them had forgotten that.

"I think he's learned from his mistakes. Did I tell you I actually heard him laughing with Skye the other day?"

"And the stars didn't fall out of the sky?" Maggie said.

"I know. Shocked me, too."

They lapsed into a comfortable silence for a few minutes. Jade finished her tea and waited for Maggie to speak again. She had the feeling her friend wasn't finished questioning her plan.

"You're sure you don't want to talk to them first?" Maggie asked eventually.

"I'm sure. Whatever is going on with them, they need to deal with it. I get the feeling I somehow set off a chain of events neither of them wanted to deal with. I just don't know what the *fraxx* the issue is."

"Striker doesn't either. Apparently, the cyborg gossip mill is in overdrive over it, though. There's a lot of speculation, but that's all it is. Wreck and Ruin have shut off all their internal links, too. I think some of the cyborgs want to head over to their cabin to talk about it, but none of them know where it is."

"Striker does, though."

"Striker and a few others, like Axe. None of them are going to tell anyone the location. So whatever is going on, your guys aren't talking about it with anyone."

"All the more reason for me to leave them alone for now. I feel like I owe them an apology, even though I have no idea why it's such a big deal that Thrash looks like them."

"Reamus Station was a brutal place, and some of the things they did to the cyborgs..." Maggie shook her head. "Striker only told me some of it, but it's horrifying."

Jade sat back and sighed as a wave of regret struck. "Do you think we'll be okay? Me and the guys, I mean."

"If Striker and I can figure it out, you can, too. Hopefully without anyone getting abducted this time."

"Once was enough for a lifetime," Jade agreed.

Maggie got the vague expression she often wore when someone was sending her a message via her internal link. She'd had one implanted so she could speak with Striker and the other rangers.

"Striker wants you home?" Jade asked.

"Yep. He's on his way over so he can walk me back." Maggie grinned and rose from her seat. "I'll see you tomorrow at the med-center. You're not going to do this alone."

They hugged, and Jade walked her best friend to the door. "I wasn't going to ask. But... thank you. It will be nice to know you'll be there when I wake up."

"There's nowhere else I'd rather be. Now, get some sleep. Medi-bots or not, you're going to need it."

"You're right. Hopefully that herbal tea you made me drink works its magic."

Jade stayed with Maggie until Striker arrived and then waved as the pair set off together. "Take care of her!" she called.

"You know I will," Striker replied, his arm already draped possessively around Maggie's waist.

Once she was alone, Jade placed the mugs in the cleaning unit and spent a few minutes tidying up the place. Despite what she'd said to Maggie, there wasn't a snowball's chance in a super nova she would sleep much tonight. Too much was weighing on her mind... and her heart.

13

———

"Are we going to talk about what happened yet? Or are you still too pissed off to be rational?" Wreckage demanded. They were racing through the woods, both of them running near their top speed despite the darkness.

"Guess," Ruin snarled. He leaped over a fallen log and crashed into the underbrush on the other side without slowing down.

"We've been doing this for hours. You do realize that running away from your problems is supposed to be a figure of speech, not a literal response. Right?" Wreckage kept pace with his batch-brother but tried to avoid the larger obstacles instead of hurtling himself over and through them.

"I'm not running *away* from anything. We're running in a loop around the cabin."

"Nope. I'm running in circles and you're running

away. Neither activity is useful." Wreckage slowed his pace and waited to see what Ruin did. The bastard kept going. Wreckage stopped and listened to his brother crash through the underbrush. The sound decreased for a while but then got louder again, accompanied by a string of profanity in every language Ruin knew... which was all of them.

"You done?" Wreckage asked once Ruin was in sight.

"You're an asshole. Have I mentioned that lately?"

"Only about nine times in the last minute or so. You want to do this here or back at the cabin?" Like most cyborgs, their night vision was enhanced to the point they could see each other clearly despite the fact that both of Liberty's moons were hidden behind clouds.

"Here. I have a feeling I'm going to need to run again once we're done." Ruin leaned against the trunk of a nearby tree, but didn't say anything else.

Fine. If he wasn't going to talk, he would have to listen instead.

"You *fraxxed* things up royally today. We both know that. What I want to hear from you is how you plan on fixing it."

"Me? How is this my fault? I'm not the one who keeps going into town where anyone can see us. I'm not the one who told me to meet you two in the tavern instead of at Jade's door. I told you this would happen if we didn't stay away." Ruin slammed his fist into the trunk behind him hard enough to send wood chips and bark flying.

"Is that what you're pissed about? That someone finally realized Thrash looks like the two of us?" Wreckage stalked forward until he was in Ruin's face. "You *fraxxing* moron. I don't care about that. I'm talking about *Jade*."

The silence was followed by a low growl of frustration. "I don't know how to fix that. I don't even know if we can. Do you think she's going to want to be with us once she finds out the truth?"

"Truth?" Wreckage felt like he was missing something. The two of them never talked about the secret they carried. It had always been easier to ignore it. Now, he wasn't sure that had been a good idea. He'd always assumed they felt the same way about the way their DNA had been used. They'd been made fathers without any say in the matter. Worse, they'd been forced to watch their offspring fight and kill each other. The worst part for him had been not knowing which ones were his. The guards only told them after one died. They'd saunter over to the cell they shared, grin, and gleefully tell them, "That was one of yours."

With some, it was obvious, like Thrash. But others resembled their other donors, including their batch-sisters. Shatter and Splinter had been clones. They'd lived through the wars only to die at the hands of the sick sons of bitches on Reamus who harvested their eggs to use to create more cyborgs. They'd died trying to protect one of their offspring. It had been stupid and pointless and doomed to fail, but they tried anyway, even knowing it would be futile and fatal.

"We failed them." It took Ruin so long to answer Wreckage had almost forgotten what they were talking about. Shatter and Splinter had made their choice and gone out fighting. How could they have failed the two women?

"What?" he asked.

"We failed them," Ruin repeated. "The cyborgs who carry our DNA. We should have found a way to escape. To protect them. Something. They're our responsibility, and we failed."

Responsibility? He'd never thought of it that way. They'd had no say in the process. How could they take responsibility for any of their offspring? They were created in a lab and grown in maturation tanks, emerging as fully grown and functional adults with behavior mods and programming instead of a childhood. "We didn't fail them. There was no escape. You know that."

"We failed, and they'll hate us for it."

"Hate us? Maybe. But not because we didn't find a way to escape. It will be because we're the reason they exist. All the suffering they endured is because of us."

Ruin stared at him. "Is that what you think?"

"I thought we both felt that way. I didn't realize."

"Neither did I." Ruin smacked the tree again, taking out another chunk of wood.

"You keep that up and it will crash down on your head, and I'm not going to yell 'timber' this time."

Ruin's laughter was raw and bitter, but it was a laugh all the same. "'Hey, asshole,' would probably work, too. Or maybe just 'tree'!"

Wreckage decided to push on with what he needed to say. "They were going to figure it out eventually. No matter how much we stayed away, they'd have noticed. We're going to live for hundreds of years, Ruin. It was just a matter of time."

"I didn't think it would happen if we stayed away."

"They're cyborgs. If an ordinary human like Jade could see it, it's sort of embarrassing that the highly enhanced and observant cyborgs missed it this long."

Another bitter laugh. "True. And that brings us back to Jade. We've always been her protectors. What will she think when she finds out we couldn't even protect our own flesh and blood?"

"I don't see it the same way you do. She's not with us because we're her protectors. She's with us because she wants to be. And I sure as hell want to be with her. Only, I don't know if she'll be interested after what you did today."

"I didn't mean to."

"I know. She knows. But it happened. If I hadn't been there, she'd have fallen, and I'm not sure you would have even noticed. That's how the mercs treated her. Like a thing to be dragged around and mutilated for their amusement." The second the words were out of his mouth, he knew they were true, even though he'd not even considered it until now. Not consciously, anyway.

"*Fraxx*. I really messed this up. I mean, I knew that. But... it's worse than I thought." Ruin scrubbed a hand through his hair and then slapped the tree behind him.

"Uh huh. Which brings us back to the question. How do we fix this?"

"Flowers aren't going to work this time. Are they?" Ruin asked.

"Not on their own. No. But it might be a good way to start. It's late, and she'll be sleeping by now." Wreckage was putting together a plan even as he spoke.

"Tomorrow, after she's done with work, we'll go see her and apologize."

"And tell her everything," Ruin said.

"No more secrets," Wreckage agreed.

"Then we need to deal with the others." Ruin didn't sound thrilled, but at least he wasn't beating up the tree anymore.

"One crisis at a time. Jade first. The others have gone this long. They can wait one more day." At least, he hoped they would.

Ruin seemed to feel the same way. "In case they don't see it that way, maybe we should leave our links offline until after we've seen Jade."

"Good idea." Wreckage turned in the direction of

their cabin. "You coming in, or do you need to log a few more miles?"

"I'll take another lap and then head in. But only if you promise we are done talking about our feelings."

"We're done. For today. Tomorrow, though..."

Ruin grunted. "Yeah. But Jade's worth it."

"Yes, she is." He just hoped that after today, she felt the same about them.

They were supposed to be in Haven for training today, but neither of them went. If they showed their faces in the colony, they'd be peppered with questions and demands for explanations they weren't ready to deal with. Not until they'd put things right with Jade.

Ruin grimaced. He'd *fraxxed* that up royally.

After Wreckage had gone back to the cabin, Ruin hadn't run another loop through the woods. He'd snuck into Haven with a bouquet of handpicked flowers and left them by her door. She'd know who left them for her, and he needed to do *something*.

He'd sent her a message she'd see when she woke up in the morning.

I'm sorry. I promised to treat you like a goddess and I didn't. No excuses. No justifications. Just heartfelt regret at what I did. I hope you can forgive me.

Ru.

He'd even signed it with the nickname she'd given

him. No one else, not even his batch-siblings, had dared to shorten his name and turn it into an endearment. Only Jade had done that. Only Jade made him happy. If she didn't forgive him… did that mean he wouldn't be happy again? Veth. Had he ruined things for Wreckage, too?

"Hell of a time to live up to my name," he muttered to himself as he jogged through the woods. They'd decided to go on patrol today instead of training, which meant they needed to swing by Axe's cabin to let him know.

He was already working when they arrived. They heard the sound of the chainsaw long before they got to his place.

"Furniture or a sculpture?" Wreckage asked. "I'm betting it's furniture."

Ruin shook his head. "He doesn't use the chainsaw much when he's making furniture. He's working on something artsy."

Wreckage snickered. "You use that word around him, and he'll use that saw on you. Artsy is not a word that really applies to Axe."

"No kidding."

They made certain to arrive with more noise than usual and approached by walking through the largest part of the clearing around the cabin to give Axe plenty of time to see them. The solitary cyborg didn't appreciate uninvited guests.

Once they were in view, Axe powered down the saw and came out to greet them. "You lost?"

"Just passing through," Wreckage said.

"We're skipping training today. On patrol instead," Ruin added.

"Thought maybe you could relay that information to Striker for us," Wreckage said.

Axe nodded. "I can do that. You might want to check water levels upriver from here. I heard from Raze last night. They were having a hell of a storm in the valley."

"Which means flash floods for him, and high water for us once the flow reaches us," Wreckage said.

"Yup. I was going to swing by on my way to training, but if the two of you do it, I could spend that time working here. I've got a few orders to fill by the end of the month and I've got a pet project on the go, too." He jerked his thumb toward the large, covered shed behind him. The doors were open, revealing a well-lit space full of tools and wood in various stages of transition to furnishings and other household items. This was how Axe made a living. From the selection of the tree to the final coat of wax, he created one-of-a-kind items that were in high demand all over the colony.

"What are you working on this time?" Wreckage asked.

"Ghost cat sculpture." Axe shrugged as if this wasn't anything special. "If no one buys it, I'll set it up on the edge of the clearing and see if it keeps the real ones away. *Fraxxing* beasts have been sniffing around my chickens."

"You have chickens?" Ruin was surprised.

"You don't?" Axe shook his head. "You should get some. Fresh eggs every morning and occasional meat for the stew pot. All they need is a strong fence, some grain, water, and whatever kitchen scraps you toss them."

Wreckage snorted. "If we feed them leftovers from Ruin's cooking, they'd all die in a week."

"Didn't your creators include basic cooking skills in your software?" Axe asked.

"Nope. Yours did?" Wreckage asked.

"Yeah. No idea why, but it made for decent meals anytime we were deployed to a planet with edible flora or fauna."

"Huh. I bet it did. And I bet if we look, there's a compatible upload we can use. You could actually become a decent cook, Wreck."

"I can't believe we didn't think about that until now." Wreckage looked chagrined. "Thanks for the tip, Axe."

"Welcome." The big man tugged at his beard. "Since I'm handing out advice and information today, here's another one. Whatever the *fraxx* you did yesterday, fix it. I'm sick of getting asked where your cabin is and how to find you two. Don't care what happened. Don't care how you make it stop. Just do it."

"Yeah, we're working on that. Sorry they bothered you." Ruin hated that the fallout of yesterday was already affecting others.

"And thanks for not telling them where to find us," Wreckage said.

Axe grunted and gestured around them. "We live out here for a reason. If we wanted visitors, we'd live somewhere else."

Ruin caught the hint. He and Wreckage were visitors, and it was time for them to go. "Thanks for everything. See you at the next training session."

Axe gave them a brief wave and a nod before heading back to his workshop. He was the most solitary of all the cyborgs on Liberty. All he wanted was to be left alone, and Ruin couldn't see any way that would ever change.

They stayed out all day, and the time in the woods was exactly what he needed to work through things. By the afternoon he was ready to talk again, and the two of them shared more of their feelings and fears than they'd ever done before. And now they had, he could see that talk was long overdue. While they both had regrets and guilt over what had happened, it wasn't for the same reasons. Each of them had just assumed the other felt the same way.

The only thing they completely agreed on was how

they felt about Jade, and even that had come as something of a revelation to Ruin. He knew he cared for her, but somewhere over the course of the day, he'd finally realized it was more than that. He *needed* her. Hell, he might even love her, but he couldn't be certain, because he'd never been in love before.

"*Are you brooding or thinking?*" Wreckage asked over their link. They'd just landed their hover-bikes in the alley beside the Bar None.

He turned off the engine before answering out loud. "Thinking. Maybe we should meet her at the palace gate instead of waiting for her here?"

"You really want to sit in front of the palace in plain view of everyone right now?" Menace asked.

"*Veth*. Right. That's not a good idea. Jade is our priority right now. Everyone else can wait."

They went up the stairs to her place. He was happy to see the flowers he'd left for her were gone. He'd had no message from her, though. He'd checked a few times over the day, though he'd ignored all the other messages and request for vid calls.

The two of them settled in to wait. And wait. And wait.

Ruin didn't like it. "She should be home by now."

"Yeah. Hang on. Maybe she went home early?" Wreckage went over and knocked on her door. No one answered, and neither of them heard anyone moving around inside.

"She might have stopped for food?" Wreckage said a few seconds later.

"Maybe." Ruin still didn't like it. Some gut instinct was insisting he find her. *Right now.*

Wreckage must have felt the same way. "We need a new plan. Waiting here for her to show up feels wrong."

Ruin didn't bother to reply. He just vaulted over the deck's railing and dropped to the alley where they'd parked. Wreckage followed less than two seconds later.

That's when the door to the tavern's kitchen opened and Saral rushed outside. "Where have you *bakaffas* been? Everyone is looking for you!"

"We were out on patrol, and now we're here to see Jade. We'll deal with everyone else later. Do you know where she is?" Wreckage asked.

The Vardarian female threw up her hands as her scales tightened in anger or frustration, making her gleam a brilliant gold. "They're looking for you *because* of Jade! Something happened during the surgery. She asked that you be contacted if things went wrong."

Dread flooded his veins with ice and left him stunned. Jade had the procedure done. Without telling them. And now—now the worst had happened.

"Is she alive?" Wreckage asked.

Saral shook her head as tears rolled down her cheeks. "I don't know. She was last I heard. The word went out about half an hour ago. Everyone is looking for you, but you've been out of contact."

She swiped at her tears and then pointed. "She's at the med-center. Hurry!"

"I know the way. Thank you." Wreckage turned and sprinted out of the alley with Ruin only a few steps behind him.

"*If she's gone...*" Ruin sent. They'd been sitting on her deck waiting for her while she was at the med-center, fighting to stay alive. He hated himself right now.

"*Don't even think it. And don't blame yourself. We both agreed to keep our internal links and comms off.*"

"*Which confirms that neither of us is making good choices these days. Maybe we should let Jade be in charge going forward.*"

"*Agreed.*"

They sped through the streets of Haven so fast they were little more than a blur to anyone watching. They needed to find Jade and figure out what the hell had gone wrong.

Fear, grief, and worry tore at his heart every step of the way. One thing he knew for certain now. This much pain could only mean one thing. He was deeply in love with Jade.

Now he just had to hope he got the chance to tell her.

14

JADE WOKE UP WITH A HEADACHE, a sure sign she'd overindulged the night before. With that in mind, she cracked open one eye just enough to get a view of her immediate surroundings. *Fraxx.* Nothing looked familiar. It also looked much too clean and bright to be anywhere she was likely to wind up after a night out. No one she knew in Athens Two lived in a place like this. It looked more like a hospital.

Hospital. The word jolted her memory. Recollection came in bits and pieces. She wasn't on Earth. This was Haven, and she'd had something done at the med-center. What was it again? Oh, right. They were trying to repair the damage to her cranial implant.

Her eyes snapped open as she reached up to the data port beside her ear. At least, that's what she tried to do, but something stopped her. A quick tug of her other hand produced the same result. Was she restrained? Why?

She looked around, worried and confused. Then she saw the problem. Wreckage and Ruin sat on either side of her bed. They wore matching expressions of deep concern tinged with relief, and they were each gripping one of her hands in theirs.

Her mouth activated before her brain, and her first words were, "What are you doing here? You weren't supposed to know about this."

Dr. Clark moved into view near her head. "You can speak to them in a moment. Right now, I need you to talk to me. How are you feeling? Are you in any pain?"

"My head aches like I have a hangover. That's all."

"Good. That's good." Dr. Clark shifted her gaze to someone Jade couldn't see. "You better let the others know she's awake and talking."

Jade heard soft footsteps and the sound of a door opening. "She's awake," Loris said in hushed tones.

"She is? Good," Maggie said and then raised her voice from a whisper to a normal tone. "Welcome back, Jaybird. You scared the hell out of us." Her voice sounded raw and unsteady, like she'd been crying.

"Who's with you?" she asked.

Maggie leaned in to view and smiled. "Everyone who cares about you is here. It's standing room only in the waiting room. I'll go tell them you're awake. Next time you promise me you're not going to die, I'm going to want it in writing."

Maggie left Jade stunned. Fear fluttered in her belly. *What the hell had happened to her and how close had she come to breaking her promise?*

As if sensing her distress, Dr. Clark placed a calming hand on her shoulder. "I know you have questions, but I need you to do a few things first. Your men are going to squeeze your hands now, and I want you to tell me if you can feel it."

The doctor looked away from her to glare at her visitors. Clearly, she wasn't happy they were here. Knowing the two of them, they'd barged in and refused to leave no matter what the doctor had threatened them with. They were here for her. But how had they found out? Had Maggie broken her promise not to tell them? Why was the doctor asking her these basic things?

Her fears didn't have time to take root before she felt both her hands being squeezed. The reassuring sensation grounded her thoughts and tightened her fingers around theirs. Why they were here didn't matter. She was happy to see them. "I feel them. Both of them."

Dr. Clark exhaled softly and then nodded. "That's great. Now, I want you to wiggle your toes for me."

Jade did as she was told. "Doing it. Please tell me my toes are moving. They feel like they are."

"They are." Dr. Clark smiled at her reassuringly. "No other pain or issues?"

"I'm groggy and I have a headache. That's it. Now,

can you please tell me why everyone is so worried?" She raised her head to look at her visitors, which made her head hurt worse and caused her stomach to roll in warning, so she eased her head back onto a pillow. "And why are *they* here?"

"We had a complication." She could hear Loris but still couldn't see her, and she wasn't going to lift her head again any time soon.

"Complication? What kind? Did the procedure work or not?"

"We don't know if it worked. If you'll excuse my lack of professionalism, shit went sideways before we got that far," Dr. Clark said, her voice thick with frustration.

Wreckage and Ruin both tightened their grip on her hands but didn't say anything.

Loris picked up the story. "I've seen something like this once before. One cyber-jockey attacked a rival through the datasphere while they were undergoing an upgrade. The attack came through the medical system we were using to monitor the patient. That time, the patient died."

Loris finally moved into Jade's view. She looked weary and haggard, but she had a gleam of satisfaction in her eyes. "We had to turn off every system and do it ourselves. Haven't done that in a decade or three."

"All the systems? What about Rae? Was she part of the attack?" Jade's mind raced through possibilities and potential suspects. How had this happened? And why?

Loris nodded sadly. "She was. We had to use an override code to take her offline."

Wreckage finally spoke up. "You almost died several times, sweetling. Once Maggie learned that something was wrong, she followed your instructions and contacted us."

"We came as soon as we heard," Ruin said.

"And they've been by your side every second since they arrived, despite my attempts to get them to move back so I could do my job." Dr. Clark tried to glare at them again, but she smiled as she did it.

Jade raised her head more gingerly this time, but she managed it without triggering any warnings. Once she could see them both, she said, "You're making it hard for me to stay mad at you, but I'm glad you're here."

"If you'd told us what you planned, we'd have been here sooner," Ruin grumbled. "But you had every reason not to tell us."

"We're here, now, and we're not leaving without you," Wreckage said.

"You see what I've been dealing with? Your men are as stubborn as old Earth mules," Dr. Clark said.

"Tell me about it." Jade settled her head back onto the pillow and turned her gaze to Dr. Clark again. "So, what happens now?"

"It's late and we could all use some rest. Especially you. Healers Tariq and Perin are here and will keep an eye on you overnight. Tomorrow, we'll run more tests. I want to be sure you're one hundred percent."

"Late? How long was I out?" They'd started the procedure by mid-afternoon. She was supposed to have been awake by evening.

"Dawn is in a few hours." Dr. Clark rubbed a hand over her face before continuing. "You were attacked four times during the procedure. The first two were attempted overdoses. Whoever or whatever did this didn't seem to be aware of your medi-bots, which scrubbed the drugs from your system before they did any harm."

"It's a good thing the Vardarian healers had briefed us thoroughly on how to anesthetize someone with nanotech. It's very different from what either of us was used to and might have saved your life. We were watching you carefully for any indication the meds weren't working correctly," Loris said.

Jade set aside her reaction to the news and pushed herself to learn the rest. "What were the other two attacks?"

"The surgical microscope we used to magnify the area we were working on failed at a critical point. At the same time, something caused a power surge. The electricity arced from the surgical tool to your body." Dr. Clark's professional mask slipped for a moment, and Jade saw exhaustion and the echoes of real fear.

Fraxx. "So, why am I not dead?"

"Doc has good instincts and fast reflexes. She

withdrew the moment the microscope failed. The power arc didn't hit anything vital," Loris said and smiled at Clark.

"You were injured but nothing critical. Between the two of us and your medi-bots, the damage is already healed."

She'd come insanely close to dying, and they still didn't know if the procedure had worked. This wasn't going at all the way she'd envisioned.

"And Rae?"

"She was overseeing the procedure. Everything that went wrong was under her control. Not only did she not stop it, but she didn't give us any warning that something was wrong."

"Something corrupted her programming," Jade said with certainty.

"Or used her program as a conduit and interfered directly," Loris agreed.

"Either way, we can't risk bringing her back online until we know what happened and fix it." Jade allowed herself a moment to consider all the damage the medical program could wreak. Every patient in the colony and on the orbital plat could be at risk, including Phaedra.

"You need to warn the princess!" she said as soon as she thought of it.

"Already done, and that spymaster fellow is investigating," Loris said with a smile and a pat on her shoulder.

"You need to focus on getting yourself back to one hundred percent. It shouldn't take long. A few more hours of rest and a good meal, and then I suspect you can go home." The doctor fixed her with a stern look. "But only if you promise to rest and leave any investigation or other work to others for at least another day. You are healing quickly, but your body remembers the trauma even if you don't."

"She'll rest," Ruin said.

"We'll make sure of it," Wreckage confirmed.

Jade tried for a dramatic sigh, but it came out as more of a breathy laugh. "You two are assuming an awful lot."

"We need to talk. The best place for us to do that is somewhere private where you can rest and recover." Wreckage moved, and she felt his lips brush the back of her hand.

"Maybe." Jade wasn't giving them more than that, but she already knew they'd won this round. If they were ready to talk, she would listen and do her best to be understanding.

"How long do I need to wait before we can try the procedure again?"

"Oh! I wasn't clear. I'm sorry. We managed to get the procedure finished after we powered everything down. You can thank Loris for that. She has far more experience than I do with manual surgery. Your cranial implant has been repaired, and we were able to install the new elements we discussed."

"Plus a bonus," Loris chimed in. "I noticed you didn't have a translator or implanted communication device. Now, you have both."

"None of the other doctors wanted to risk adding new tech. I thought I'd need to get by without either. Thank you!"

"Jade has the ability to connect to the cyborg network?" Wreckage asked.

"She does. For now, we've left all those channels off. She can choose which ones to activate once she's had more rest. We can do that at the same time we test her cranial implant."

"We can do that today?" Jade asked.

"If you rest, yes," Dr. Clark said and then added, "Loris and I are certain that there's no risk to you. I can't promise that the repair will work, but if it fails, you'll be fine."

Holy fraxx. "No risk of death?"

"None. As I mentioned, Loris is skilled at this kind of work. She made sure that everything was safe and ready to go. We just wanted your permission before we went ahead."

"You have my permission and my thanks." If that's what she had to do to find out if she could be whole again, she'd find a way to stay in bed and follow the doctor's orders. Now more than ever, she needed to be at the top of her game.

Ruin spoke up. "You're sure there's no risk? What about whatever attacked her the last time?"

"I'm certain, and so is Loris. As for the reactivation, Jade will be awake. I'll inject some temporary freezing for her comfort, and we can have this done in a matter of minutes. Then she will need to rest again."

"I'll rest! I promise."

"She will do as you say, Dr. Clark," Wreckage said.

Jade lay back and let it all sink in. Someone had tried to kill her, but they'd failed. Once she had her abilities back, she'd track them down and end the threat.

Plus, she liked the idea that she, Wreckage, and Ruin could be linked. She wouldn't be left out of their conversations anymore. Part of her wanted that more than anything. But first, they needed to talk.

15

―――

"*T*HIS IS AMAZING," Jade sent to the two of them via their new internal link. It wasn't the first time she'd said this, and Ruin suspected it wouldn't be the last. He didn't care how often she said the same thing. She was alive and speaking to them. That's all that mattered.

"*Amazing doesn't cover it. This means I can talk dirty to you any time I want,*" Wreckage sent to them both.

"*Just make sure you're on the right channel. Trust me when I tell you that no one else wants to hear that outside the three of us.*"

Jade laughed out loud at that. "Definitely double-check the channel. As much as I enjoy being a bit of an exhibitionist, that would be taking it too far."

They'd taken her back to their cabin after the final

activation was done. Their place had only limited access to Haven's datasphere, which meant there was no way anyone could attack Jade that way. They could protect her here, and it was far enough from the colony that she wouldn't be tempted to try and go back to work before she was ready.

Now the three of them were on the couch in their living room—Wreckage on one side and Ruin on the other with Jade tucked in between them. At least, that's how they'd started out. At the moment, Jade's head and shoulders rested on his thighs and her legs stretched out over Wreckage.

Ruin couldn't stop touching her to reassure himself she was here. Alive, whole, and happy. His fingers played with her hair as they cuddled and talked about anything and everything but the one topic they needed to talk about.

If no one else was going to do it, he'd have to. "We need to explain what happened yesterday."

Jade nodded. "You do. But first, I need to say something." She swallowed and then spoke again. "I should have told you both that I was going to have the procedure. You deserved to know. I was pissed off at you both for keeping secrets, and I convinced myself that meant I could do it, too. I'm sorry for that."

"Don't do that again. If you had died and we hadn't been there. If we hadn't been able to even say goodbye." Ruin leaned over her so she could see him clearly. "When Saral told us what had happened, all I could think about was you, and what you mean to me. Somewhere between the tavern and the med-center, I figured out I'm in love with you. Deeply and stupidly in love. If you'd left us without ever hearing me say it…"

She reached up and touched a finger to his lips. "Stop right there. Did you just say you were stupidly in love with me? I'm not sure how to take that."

"He means he's an idiot when he's around you. Does stupid things. Says even stupider things. Please see exhibit A, his last statement." Wreckage was laughing as he spoke. The bastard.

"Yeah, that. You see? You've broken my brain, little goddess."

"And stolen our hearts," Wreckage said. "And for the record, I love you, too, and I'm pissed that Ruin said it first."

Jade laughed until tears trickled from the corners of her eyes. "What am I going to do with the two of you?"

"Put up with us for the rest of our lives?" Ruin hadn't expected to say that, and he wasn't even sure what it meant, but it felt right.

Jade stopped laughing. "Was that a proposal?"

"More of a hopeful suggestion. After all, we haven't told you our secret yet," he admitted.

"You should probably do that." Jade gave him a

tight smile that was one part encouragement and two parts worry.

"You know we were created during the Resource Wars," he said.

"But you were never freed. The two of you were sent to Reamus Research Station instead," Jade said.

"Not two. Four."

She opened her mouth to speak but then closed it again without saying a word.

Ruin continued. "Shatter and Splinter were our batch-sisters, but they were also clones."

Wreckage nodded. "Smart, like you. They were both good strategists, but when they worked together, they were brilliant."

"What happened to them?" she asked.

For a moment, the words wouldn't come, but he forced himself to keep going. He had to tell her. He *needed* to tell her. "A lot of truly terrible things happened to all four of us. We were among the first to arrive. Back then, the corporations were still trying to figure out how cyborgs had broken their control over us. They experimented on what few subjects they had to try and learn how it happened and prevent it from occurring again."

"How many of you were there in the beginning?"

"I honestly don't know. They kept us isolated from each other back then. We caught glimpses of each other as they moved us around and sometimes we'd hear one of us when they..." He broke off as the memories of that dark time swarmed up and tried to devour him.

Jade reached up to touch his cheek. "You're not there anymore, Ru. You're here with Wreck and me, and you're safe."

He exhaled slowly and turned to nuzzle her fingers. It was like she'd looked into his soul and told him the one thing he needed to hear.

"We'll do this together," Wreckage sent and picked up the story. "They'd use verbal commands to reset our conditioning and then try to push us to the point we'd break free again. They were convinced that if they could just find the trigger, they could eliminate it from future versions."

Jade frowned. "But that's not how it happened. It was a slow process for most of you. Right? And the ones who got there first helped the rest."

Wreckage's left hand closed into a fist. "Those assholes refused to believe that because it meant their whole design was fundamentally flawed. I think some of what they did was more to punish us for making them look bad than for any other reason."

"And some of us died. But not as many as you'd expect. They needed us, you see," Ruin said.

"What for?" she asked, her voice already wary, as if she was bracing for what she heard next.

"The corporations were ordered to destroy their genetic material, the research, and their labs. Without the stolen DNA samples, they needed another source."

She blanched. "You."

"Us," Ruin confirmed. "They used us to create the next generation of cyborgs on Reamus Station. We didn't know until they brought us out of isolation. They'd kept us away from the new ones in case we tried to teach them how to break free of their conditioning."

"They didn't want you corrupting their new toys with dangerous ideas." Jade's tone was venomous. "The bastards."

"Exactly. It wasn't until the techs finally realized the new cyborgs could break free of the mind control on their own that they stopped trying to isolate us. Even then, all the cyborgs created during the wars were kept in a different area from the post-war creations."

"All that time alone," Jade mused. "No wonder you're not comfortable in crowds."

"That's part of it. I think that's why Axe is such a loner. He was so violent they kept him locked down in solitary. Ruin and I spent some time that way, but not nearly so long as Axe."

"Why did they put you in solitary?" Jade asked.

"As punishment. To control us. To isolate us," Ruin said.

"And to make sure we didn't go on a rampage after Shatter and Splinter died," Wreckage said in a voice gone tight with sorrow.

"They killed them? Why? How?"

"Like Ruin said, we weren't allowed to mix with the general population, but we could see them. When another female cyborg appeared who looked almost exactly the same as Shatter and Splinter, we realized what they'd done."

"They used you all." Jade sounded horrified.

"They did. They also underestimated what the reaction would be."

"What happened?"

Ruin sucked in a ragged breath and continued the story. "You have to understand what it was like for the women. The guards and techs had... other uses for them. They could choose to be with one of us, and if they said no, that was it. The techs used the compliance codes to take that choice away from them."

"Skye told me about that. Is that how it happened? They fought back?"

"They fought, but it wasn't to protect themselves. The guards came after the new cyborg."

"Oh *fraxx*." Horrified comprehension dawned in Jade's eyes. "They tried to protect her."

Memories he'd done his best to bury rose to the surface of his mind. The screams of fury, the sound of bending steel as his sisters attacked the electrified bars of their cells, and then the stench of burning flesh. It hadn't stopped them. Not this time. Somehow, the two women had broken out of their cells and gone on the attack.

"They killed five of the bastards together. Then

Splinter went down and Shatter..." Ruin paused and Wreckage continued for him.

"Shatter went berserk. That's the only way to describe it. She killed two more guards with her bare hands, picked up one of the weapons and then went for the cyborg female. It was *fraxxing* surreal. We saw it all happen, but we couldn't do anything to stop it."

"What do you mean, she went for the cyborg?" Jade hadn't put the pieces together yet, so Wreckage explained.

"Endure or escape? That's what Shatter said to her. The other one, she was so new she didn't even have a name yet, just a number. The other one smiled and lowered her hands.

"She told Shatter she wanted to escape. Our sister put the blaster under her chin and pulled the trigger."

Tears streamed from Jade's eyes as she listened. One of her hands found Ruin's, and the other reached for Wreckage, who took it in his.

"She protected her the only way she could," Jade finally said. "I'm guessing they didn't let her live after that?"

"She made her own choice. She turned to look at us..." Wreckage broke off and looked pleadingly at Ruin.

"She was wounded, bleeding, and defiant right to the end. She turned to face us, smiled, raised that blaster, and spun around to fire at the guards as they rushed her. She was dead two seconds later."

Jade sat up, sending a fresh wave of tears coursing down her cheeks. She pulled them both to her and hugged them tightly. They hugged her right back, the three of them holding on to each other until the worst of the memories passed.

Jade finally eased up enough she could wipe her face with her hand. "That's... I don't know if there's a word for how horrific that must have been. I lost my brothers, too, but not like that."

"They were braver than we were," Ruin said.

Wreckage's jaw tightened and he shook his head. "Maybe. But they left us. I'm still a little pissed at them for that."

"You are?" Ruin thought he was the only one who felt that way. "Me too."

"Yeah? Guess we really should have talked about this before now. Huh?"

Jade shot them a look of pure disbelief. "Before now? You two haven't talked about this? Ever?"

"Not until yesterday," Ruin admitted.

"Unbelievable." Jade rolled her eyes. "But it makes me feel better to know that you're as bad at communicating with each other as you are with me."

"Actually, I think we're better with you," Wreckage said a little sheepishly.

Jade groaned. "We'll have to work on that, then. But later. For now, I'm still confused about something. Why is this all a secret? How can the others not know about your sisters or the links between some of you?"

Ruin tucked her head under his chin, not ready to let go of her yet. "Because none of the cyborgs in that generation survived for more than a year. I think they did that intentionally, to make sure the story didn't become a source of inspiration to others. I'm sure Axe knows, but he's never spoken of it. Edge might have heard stories, but he arrived later, so we don't know."

"And after that, they reinforced our cells and kept us away from the others for a long time. We could watch, but we never spoke to any of them. Not until much, much later. By then we'd grown our hair long and had beards that covered up our faces. No one ever noticed that some of the younger ones looked like us."

"You mean the ones like Thrash?" Jade asked.

"We can't be sure, but Thrash is probably a composite of the two of us. Others also share our DNA but not to the same degree," Wreckage said.

"And they have no idea?" Jade asked.

"It would come up sometimes, but we all know the DNA we're based on was stolen from the Vault of the Fallen. Some shared traits were bound to crop up, and we'd remind the others of that when it came up," Wreckage said.

Ruin continued, "That's why we don't spend too much time around the others."

"Okay, I understand how you've kept this a secret. What I don't get is why?" Jade looked from one to the other, her brow creased and her nose scrunched in confusion.

"Because once they know, they'll hate us," he said.

Jade looked stunned. "Why would they hate *you*?"

He and Wreckage answered at the same time. "Because we failed them."

"How?"

"We're the reason they exist. All their suffering is because of us," Wreckage said.

"And we couldn't protect them. In many ways, they're our children, and we seriously sucked as father figures," Ruin said.

Ruin waited for her to grasp what they'd told her. Once she understood, would she hate them, too?

"You two think..." She sighed and shook her head. "You're wrong. There's no reason to be angry at you. Never mind *hate* you."

"We failed them," Ruin repeated.

"You both said that already. Though I notice you each have a different reason why you think you failed them."

"We don't think. We know," Wreckage argued.

Jade cocked her head to one side. "Really? How did you fail them? Did you willingly hand over your DNA to the assholes on Reamus? For that matter, did you volunteer to go there in the first place?"

"No. That was done against our will," Wreckage said.

"So how is it your fault that the other cyborgs exist? You had nothing to do with it."

"But we're their progenitors," Wreckage said. But a

note of doubt now surfaced in his voice that hadn't been there before.

"You are. And that means something. But it doesn't mean you're their parents. You didn't agree to any part of what was done to you."

Jade turned to look at Ruin. "And your theory that they'll hate you because you didn't help them escape isn't any better. The two of you were prisoners. You think you had two choices—endure or escape."

He flinched when she used the same words Shatter had that day, but Jade wasn't finished. "The way I see it, that's a false choice. There was no way for any of you to escape. You were on a *fraxxing* space station in the middle of empty space. Your only choice was to live or to die. Your sisters made their choice. You made a different one. No one is going to hate you for that. They all made the same choice you did. They lived!" Jade's voice rose as she delivered her final words.

Wreckage looked stunned, which was exactly how Ruin felt. He kept trying to find an argument that would prove Jade wrong, but he couldn't come up with one.

"And for the record, I'm very glad the two of you decided to live. If you hadn't, we would have never met, and I wouldn't have fallen in love with you both."

The sudden change of topic knocked Ruin off balance. "You love us?"

"I do. Very much. Even though you're both clearly allergic to discussing your feelings and very attached to your own opinions." She laughed softly and kissed his cheek before leaning over to kiss Wreckage.

"So, you're not angry?" Wreckage asked.

"About all of this? No. About the fact you two have been keeping this toxic secret from the other cyborgs for so long? Hell yes. You have to tell them. And yeah, they're going to be mad that you never mentioned this before because if I've learned one thing about the cyborgs here, they want to *belong*. You have an entire family out there who don't know it yet."

"Family," Ruin uttered the word slowly, testing the way it felt.

"Yes. Family." Jade gave him a look that was one part amusement and one part frustration. "They don't need fathers, or even father figures. They're all grown adults. But you could kick Thrash's ass and teach him some manners. Maybe some better lines, too. That one needs all the help he can get."

Everything she said made sense, but it would take some time for him to absorb it. He'd been so certain of everything, including the fact that he and Wreckage felt the same way. Only they didn't. They'd felt guilty for different reasons, and now Jade had come along and blasted both their beliefs to dust.

"See?" Wreckage said. "I told you we should let Jade be in charge."

Jade laughed, and suddenly everything felt right in Ruin's world. "That's the best idea I've heard all day.

My first act of leadership is to declare that it's time for us to go to bed."

"You're tired? Why didn't you say you needed rest?" Ruin demanded.

The look she gave them was hot enough to melt hull plating. "Who said anything about resting?"

16

Jade laughed as Ruin scooped her into his arms and
rose, the two cyborgs racing to the nearest bedroom,
which happened to be Ruin's. Their beds were too
small for all three of them to sleep together, so they'd
taken to alternating bedrooms. She'd sleep with the
room's owner while the other one would sleep alone.
Something told her that would change soon.

The joy and relief she felt after their talk made her
almost giddy. She'd been prepared for some dark and
terrible secret that would ruin any chance of a future
for the three of them. While the truth had been worse
than anything she'd imagined, it wasn't what she'd
expected. Grief and guilt had twisted in her lovers'
hearts and convinced them they were to blame for
things they had no control over. It would take time for
those wounds to heal, but now the truth was out in the
light, she believed healing *would* happen. Not just for

them but for her, too. They'd find their way through this together.

Her lovers had clearly had enough talking because they didn't say a word as Ruin set her down on the floor beside his bed.

Wreckage caught hold of her hands and lifted her arms over her head as Ruin raised her shirt just enough to bare her breasts. He took a moment to kiss and nuzzle each nipple before raising the shirt higher, but then he stopped again once the fabric covered her face.

He slipped a finger under the collar, moving it just enough to free her mouth. She was caught between their big bodies, her hands still over her head when Ruin kissed her. His mouth was as hot as a brand, but his lips were gentle as they moved over hers.

Liquid heat flooded her veins and pooled deep in her core as she kissed him back. He moved away too soon, and she rose on her toes to chase his mouth when the kiss ended.

"You're supposed to be resting and recovering," Wreckage whispered in her ear. "Let us take care of you, sweetling."

"You're our goddess," Ruin stated as he pulled the shirt up over her head. "And it's time for worship."

A thrill of desire chased down her spine as she looked up into Ruin's heated gaze, and she realized something was still left unsaid between them.

She reached out to them both, one hand on Wreckage's hip and the other on Ruin's chest. "I don't need to be worshipped. I want to be with the two men I love with all my heart."

"It's official. You're ours." Wreckage pressed an open-mouthed kiss to her bare shoulder. Ruin simply stared at her for several heartbeats before dropping his head to kiss her hard.

Wreckage laughed. "Good job, you rendered him speechless."

"I'm not speechless, asshole. I'm enjoying the moment," Ruin replied with a hint of a snarl.

Jade burst out laughing. As far as she was concerned, this was the *real* moment. It summarized what her life would be like from now on. Love, laughter, and rumbles of annoyance as the men she loved growled at each other. It wasn't what some women would want. To her? It was perfect.

They shed the rest of their clothes slowly, stopping to touch and tease each other so often that by the time she managed to kick free of her socks, she was trembling and breathless with need.

They guided her to the bed, settling her in the middle with each of them claiming a side. Ruin leaned over and kissed her once more before coaxing her to roll onto her side so she faced away from him.

Wreckage claimed her mouth next, his tongue tangling with hers as he cupped her cheek in one callused hand. The three of them had been together almost every night since her first visit, but this time was different. She was too lost in desire and love to spend time trying to fathom what it was, only that this felt like *more*.

She wrapped her fingers around Wreckage's cock, stroking it from root to tip. His groans vibrated against her tongue as they kissed. Ruin nipped and nuzzled at her ear and neck, his hand curving around to toy with her breasts.

When he pressed one of his thighs between her legs, she opened for him, her entire body trembling as he moved his hand down her flank to her hip and then her thigh. He guided her top leg upward and back until it was draped over his muscular thigh.

Wreckage made a low sound of male approval and cupped her pussy in one big hand, his fingers stroking through her already wet flesh.

"Our lady always comes first," Ruin said, his hand reclaiming its place on her breast.

"Always," Wreckage agreed. His fingers slipped inside her, the pad of his thumb seeking out her throbbing clit as his thick fingers moved into her channel.

She bucked and moaned as pleasure bloomed inside her, riding his fingers as he fucked her with slow, deliberate motions.

"That's right, little goddess. Tell us how good it feels. We want to hear you."

She moaned loudly, and Wreckage increased the pace of his seduction. Was this the game? The louder she was, the more they rewarded her?

Jade grinned to herself. This was a game with no losers.

With her next soft cry, Ruin joined in, his fingers toying with her nipples. He pinched and rolled the sensitive nubs, sending jolts of electric ecstasy straight to her clit.

Soon she was drunk with pleasure, every touch sending her closer to the brink of release, and every sound she made only increased the sensations flooding her body.

She shuddered once and then stiffened as she orgasmed, crying out their names as she let waves of pleasure sweep her away.

By the time she came back to full awareness, Wreckage had eased his cock out of her hands and moved down the bed so he was positioned just outside her entrance, the thick crown already wet with her juices.

Ruin had moved her leg higher up his thigh, opening her wider. Then, she caught the scent of *uli* oil. They had introduced her to it earlier, and the citrusy, spicy aroma told her exactly what they had planned. The lubricant made her skin tingle in the most pleasurable of ways, and now Ruin drizzled some of it over her backside, using his fingers to spread it between her cheeks.

"Ready?" Ruin asked.

"Yes." She was more than ready.

Wreckage kissed her softly. "Remember, all you have to do is relax and let us love you."

She laughed. "I think I can manage that."

Ruin eased a well-lubed finger into her back channel, the sting quickly morphing into a pleasurable tingle as the *uli* oil worked its magic.

Wreckage rolled his hips several times, teasing her with the head of his cock. She grabbed his hip and pulled him closer, making her need clear.

"You're not in control here, sweetling," he reminded her before kissing her senseless, his mouth cutting off any retort she might have come up with. Wreckage finally entered her, sliding his cock into her channel until he was buried to the hilt.

Her inner walls fluttered around him as he groaned against her lips. He thrust into her several more times before catching hold of her upper leg and drawing it up over his leg near his hip.

The change in angle allowed his shaft to stroke along her clit with each thrust while opening her up to Ruin.

"Perfect," Ruin said, withdrawing his fingers.

"And ours," Wreckage said, holding her leg against his before plundering her mouth with a kiss so sultry and hot that she almost forgot to breathe.

A heartbeat later, the head of his cock pressed against her back entrance, and she forced herself to relax despite the anticipation thrumming through her. When Wreckage withdrew again, Ruin entered, claiming her with slow, shallow thrusts, each one a little deeper than the last.

She couldn't have moved if she wanted to, so she clung to her lovers and let them take her higher than she'd ever been before. Her body full, her heart overflowing, she gave voice to everything she felt, her cries blending with the sounds of sex and the groans of her lovers.

They worked her in unison, and for once, she didn't mind that they were communicating via their link without including her. Desire sizzled in her veins as another orgasm started to build. Every motion made her gasp while every thrust and counterthrust drew her deeper into the maelstrom of desire. She flexed her inner walls around them over and over, milking their cocks as she teetered at the edge of her control.

One more thrust from Wreckage was all it took. Her senses shattered into shards of crystalline bliss as both men groaned and came a moment later.

Jade regained her senses slowly, surprised to find her lashes wet with tears. She felt complete and content in ways she'd never thought possible.

Eventually, her lovers rose to clean up. Then they returned to the bed, the two of them washing and drying her body as she lounged, languid and sated.

Ruin stretched out beside her, drawing her up against the hard warmth of his body. "Sleep, Jade. I'll be right here, watching over you."

She nodded but looked around until she saw

Wreckage. He was getting dressed again. "And where will you be?"

"Watching over you both," Wreckage said. "Sleep, sweetling."

She closed her eyes and let herself drift off into the deepest, most perfect sleep of her life. She was safe. She was whole. She was loved. And tomorrow, she'd track down whatever was threatening her home and put an end to it.

17

———

ON A NORMAL DAY, the room where Jade and her teammates worked felt spacious and quiet, but today was different. The air hummed with tension, most of it coming from the two cyborgs flanking her as they entered. Wreckage and Ruin were in gargoyle mode, but for once, she didn't mind. They just wanted to protect her, and given what she'd gone through lately, she'd be foolish to argue. Someone or something had tried to kill her once already.

Dr. Clark and Loris stood out of the way, their portable med kits open and ready in case anything unexpected happened when she jacked in for the first time.

The doctor greeted them warmly, but she didn't look entirely happy. "For the record, when I said we could try activating the implant today, I thought we'd be doing it in the med-center. Are you certain this is wise?"

"Wise?" Jade shrugged. "Probably not. It is necessary, though. Now we know this thing is real and a threat, it has to be terminated. I'm the only one with the skills and hardware to go deep enough into the datasphere to do that."

Dr. Clark nodded once. "Loris said you'd say that."

Jade grinned at the installer. "Loris knows my kind. We're all as stubborn as we are crazy."

Yardan and Skye entered at that moment, filing into the room with two unexpected additions. Allax and his anrik, Lorn.

Jade's filters failed as she caught sight the male she suspected might be working against the colony's interests. "What is *he* doing here?"

"No," Ruin snarled and moved to place himself between Allax and Jade.

Yardan shot Ruin a look of pure challenge that did nothing to lower the tension. "Yes. They're with me."

Skye uttered a soft laugh and placed her hand on Yardan's chest, soothing the spymaster. "What Yardan meant to say was that Allax and Lorn are *working* with us."

Jade's mouth fell open, but before she could ask follow-up questions, Yardan turned to glare at his mate. "It's not much of a *secret* spy network if you tell others about it."

"Vin," she said, her voice low but firm. "Everyone in this room was fully vetted and cleared. You should know that since you're the one who did the vetting. They need to know."

Vin? Jade wanted to ask about the spymaster's odd nickname but decided now wasn't the time. "Are you saying Allax is a spy?"

The Vardarian in question took his anrik's hand and then answered for himself. "I'm a distant cousin of the ruling family of Vardaria and a member of their court."

"A *very* distant cousin," Lorn chimed in. "Thank all the winds that blow."

"When Prince Tyran announced the diaspora, the empress wasn't pleased. She had her spymaster speak to me about sending in discreet reports about the new colony and her brother's actions." He shifted his wings in the Vardarian version of a shrug. "I agreed to do it."

"Like he had any choice," Lorn muttered. "But it worked out since we both *wanted* to come to Haven."

Jade's gaze dropped to the male's linked hands. "You love each other," she said with a smile.

"We do," Allax confirmed. "I'll admit we weren't sure how you'd feel about that, so we were being discreet until we got to know you better."

"I thought the two of you bickered like a married couple already. This just confirms it. I take it Empress Neha doesn't know?"

"About us? No. She'd shed her scales if she did. If she knew that I went to Yardan and told him what she wanted me to do the moment we broke orbit, she'd exile me."

"You're a double agent," Wreckage said. "You feed the empress what Yardan wants her to know."

The spymaster nodded. "And he does a fine job of it."

"If you're on team Haven, why were you so unhappy when the princess made her announcement the other day?" Jade asked.

"Because it's likely he's not the only spy the empress sent. He has to look and act the part she assigned him, or one of the others might get suspicious."

"And you don't know who the others are," Ruin stated.

"I have a fair idea, but that's a different conversation." Yardan scowled at them. "One you are not cleared for."

"This is what you meant when you told me that things were being handled?" Jade asked.

"It is. I couldn't say anything more, as we weren't in a secure location. For obvious reasons, none of you can talk about this outside this room." Yardan glanced over at the doctor and the medic. "This is one of those things I told you we'd discuss later."

"Only one of them?" Loris asked with a smile. "I

love this place more each day. Fresh air, gorgeous scenery, and just a hint of intrigue."

Yardan looked at her askance. "I can't tell if you're joking or not."

Everyone laughed, and some of the tension left the room.

Jade enjoyed the lull and then returned to the work at hand. "What about Rae? Do we know what happened to her?"

Skye answered. "They're doing a line-by-line review of her code to be sure she's clean and safe to restart. The preliminary report indicates a high probability that it wasn't a coding issue. They think something literally took over her program and used her like a puppet. Rae's program was only recently added to the Hub's system. That connect allowed the ghost to take her over."

Jade had expected this, but hearing it confirmed still sent a chill down her spine. "Our ghost is complex enough to have possessed her program. That's what I suspected, and it's disturbing. Someone is using an AI so advanced it has to be in violation of the Pinocchio Protocol."

Yardan nodded. "That's the name of the law this part of the galaxy uses to ensure that artificial intelligences are compliant, non-dangerous, and non-sentient. Yes?"

"Yes," Jade said. "This ghost might be sentient, or it might not, but it still tried to kill me. That's reason enough to destroy it. The bigger question is, who the *fraxx* programmed it?"

A hologram appeared near the center of the room. Jade hadn't noticed the projector discreetly installed in the ceiling until now.

"Who programmed it?" Phaedra asked, even before her digital avatar had come into focus. "I'll give you three guesses and the first two don't count."

Jade and several others greeted the new arrival.

"You safe?" Jade asked her.

"Safe, bored, and pissed off." Phaedra's expression was stormy.

"In this case, bored is good. Would destroying this digital ghost improve your mood?"

"Definitely, but I won't be happy until we've dealt with these assholes for good."

"You think it's the Gray Men?" Jade asked. The Gray Men had been a shadowy cabal whose members included some of the wealthiest corporate owners in the galaxy, along with a mixture of scientists, politicians, and operatives. They had funded the development of the cyborg program, tested drugs on unknowing populations, and committed countless illegal and immoral acts in the quest for absolute power. That quest had failed with many of the members dead or in custody, but not everyone had been caught, or even identified.

Phaedra's lip curled with disgust. "We believe it's

the Shadows. Think of them as the Grays two-point-oh, now with more xenophobia."

The Shadows. It made a terrible kind of sense, but Jade didn't know much more about them than their name. Not that it mattered right now. She didn't need to know who they were or what they wanted. All she had to do was hunt down and destroy their latest creation.

"Before I go in, I need to ask you something. Do you have a theory as to why you never saw this ghost? And why it never manifested itself in Rae until now? Surely it could have gone after other targets."

Phaedra inclined her head. "I have a theory or two. I think the most likely reason is that it was avoiding me. I'm the only one on this planet who can fully enter the datasphere. If I'd seen any signs of it, I'd have hunted it down. Neither Allax nor Lorn can go deep enough to detect it, especially if they didn't know to look for something like that. As far as I can tell, you didn't see any evidence of this thing until after I left. Whatever information it had, it didn't know you could still connect to the datasphere, even if the connection was far lighter than mine."

"That would explain why it didn't know about your medi-bots, either," Dr. Clark said. "You got yours far earlier than normal because of your injuries, but that information is only in your medical file, which is heavily encrypted. If this ghost didn't have full access to Rae's programing, it wouldn't have been able to read your file. At least, that's how I think it would work."

"You're right. That would explain a few things," Phaedra agreed. "But it did know you went for an appointment and could have overheard your conversation about repairing your implants. If you were fully functional, it wouldn't be able to hide from you, so it attacked."

Jade raised her chin and squared her shoulders. "It missed its shot. Now, I'm coming after it."

"Kick its ass, Slyce," Phaedra said, using her cyber-jockey name.

"Slyce?" Ruin asked.

"I'll explain later. Right now, I have a digital ghost to kill." Jade walked to her desk but didn't sit down in the cybernetically linked chair she'd used before. If this worked, she wouldn't need it anymore. The thought made her smile. She was back!

Still grinning, she selected a standard style chair and started to drag it over to her desk. Wreckage made a tsking sound, stepped in, and lifted the entire thing with one hand. "Where do you want this?"

"Right there." She pointed. "And then you can flex your sexy biceps and move that other chair out of the way."

"That one stays." Ruin settled himself into the chair and began strapping himself in. "Jade, show me how this works."

She should have expected this, but it still caught

her by surprise. "You've never been in cyberspace, Ru. You can't help me in there."

His eyes met hers. "You don't need my help. You need my protection." He gave her a lopsided grin. "Besides, you know how much I love new experiences."

"Yeah, about as much as a *peskin* loves water," Jade said. As she spoke, she placed the cranial interface on his head, taking a moment to adjust it to fit him."

Yardan frowned. "What's a *peskin?*"

"They're beautiful, vicious little creatures that sink like a stone if they enter the water," Skye explained.

Jade fitted the interactive gloves to Ruin's hands and then leaned in to kiss him. "Inside, you'll still feel like you have a body, but that's an illusion. Our digital avatars are made up of energy and data, just like everything else in the datasphere. To me, it feels like flying through a cityscape. Others see it more like an ocean they swim through. Go with whatever your mind decides is real. Reality is more like a filter your brain chooses for you. Everyone is a little different."

"So we won't see the same things?" If he couldn't perceive threats, how could he protect her?

"We'll see it differently, and I will see much farther and in more detail than you, but both of us will know a threat when we see it." She winked at him. "Trust me, big guy. All you need to do is follow me."

"I'll follow you to the ends of the universe," he said

softly. "Wreckage will stay here to protect your physical body. I'll watch your digital one."

"Love you," she said and then moved to her own chair. "Love you too, Wreck."

He blew her a kiss and winked. "Go kick some digital ass, sweetling."

She settled back in the chair, took a long, deep breath, and plugged the cord into her cranial data port. For one long second, she wondered if it would work... and then she wasn't in her body anymore. She was back in the datasphere.

She was home, and this time, she wasn't alone.

Wreckage had shared his stored files on his one experience in the datasphere, so Ruin had some idea what to expect. It was still so much more than he'd been prepared for. It was a surreal place full of activity, yet it was also peaceful. There was a solitude to it he hadn't expected, and a beauty that was beyond imagining.

Wreckage's version of the space was similar in some ways and wildly different in others. Jade's point about each person's mind translating things into their own unique version of reality was demonstrated everywhere.

To Ruin, this looked like a crystalline forest, their roots forming networks that intersected and curled around each other. Lights pulsed along the roots, some continuing into the distance while others flowed into the massive trunks of trees.

Leaves every color of the rainbow glowed as they danced in a wind he couldn't perceive while rivers flowed in three dimensions. The ribbons of lights moved through the roots, the tree trunks, and up into what he saw as an open sky of the deepest blue that went on for eternity.

"Can you hear me?" Jade's voice seemed to come from his left, and he turned toward the sound that wasn't sound at all. He spotted her avatar, which was more of a Jade-shaped shadow in this world. She was made up of the same myriad of colors and pulsing lights as the rest of this place, only compressed into a form he could recognize and outlined in the same deep blue as the sky.

Then he realized what this meant. She was here in the datasphere, alive and well. "It worked! You're here!"

She laughed and spun in place, the movement making her avatar sparkle and surge with new colors. "I'm back! Welcome to my world."

"I like it here. Do I look like you do? A shadowy shape?"

"You do. Though I think you're actually bigger in here. That's interesting. I'll need to investigate why once we're back in reality."

"Are we speaking through our internal channel?" he asked.

"No. I've created a new link between us. It will only last until we leave."

She spread her arms, gesturing around them. "I have missed this so much. I hope you'll come back with me another time. There's so much I want to show you and Wreckage. But for now... we have work to do."

"And my job is to keep you safe." He felt for the weapons he'd been wearing and discovered they were missing. *Fraxx.* "How can I do that if I don't have weapons?"

"You *are* a weapon, Ru. All you have to do is envision what you want and it will manifest. Reality is what we make of it, here more than anywhere else. Basically, all you need to remember is that this is a digital world. Everything here is composed of the same thing—energy and data."

She opened her hand, palm up. For a moment, her hand was empty, and then several butterflies appeared on her fingertips. They took flight and settled into a circular pattern above her head. "See?"

He nodded and raised one hand, imagining what he wanted. A long shaft that looked like a shadowy version of his kes'tarv appeared, and he gripped it firmly. It felt exactly like the real thing, down to the weight and balance.

"I think I like it here," he said, giving the weapon a twirl to test it.

Jade floated around to face him. "This is my sanctuary. The one place where I am in control." The butterflies grew larger and then exploded into shimmering sparks that fell around her like rain and were reabsorbed into her body.

He understood now. She thought of cyberspace the way he thought of the forest, and she'd been denied access to her sanctuary. She hadn't known if she would ever be able to return. If he'd been in her place, he'd have done exactly what she had. Risks be damned.

"Your sanctuary is beautiful. I see why you missed it." He wished away the weapon, knowing he could recall it when it was needed. "Let's evict your would-be assassin and make this place safe again."

Jade took the lead, soaring over the crystalline forest and weaving her way through the rivers that flowed in whirling loops of light. She seemed to know exactly where to go, so he settled in behind her, using all his senses to scan this strange realm.

"You said I'd know a threat when I saw it. How?" he asked.

"Your mind will sense it because it will be different from the rest of this place. This datasphere is made up mostly of Vardarian tech, which is crystal based. We're certain the ghost is a corporation construct, so it won't look like everything else. I think it's learned to camouflage itself to a certain extent, but it can't hide itself from me anymore."

"So, I need to look for something that doesn't belong?" he asked.

"Exactly."

After a time, Jade descended, leading him through the canopy of digital leaves and into the forest below. She approached a massive tree and placed a hand against the trunk. "Do you see it?"

He shook his head. "I see a tree, but that's not what you mean."

"A tree?" She laughed. "Of course you'd see a tree. I should have guessed that's what your brain would choose as a filter. Look closely at this *tree*. What's different about it?"

It took him almost a minute to see what she meant. "Some of the flashes of light are almost black. More like the light is being blocked or suppressed somehow."

"You do see it!" She cocked her head and looked thoughtful. "That's interesting, too. You shouldn't be able to. Something about your cyborg implants must be helping you. Remind me to talk to Phaedra about that when we're back. I think we need to convince more cyborgs to join the team."

"So, what am I looking at?"

"For want of a better term? This is the site of the infection. The place our ghost considers home."

To him, it still looked like a tree. "Where is it? I mean, what system?"

"This is part of the Hub's network. Whoever introduced this thing into our datasphere did it here."

That made sense to him. They knew one of the Shadows' agents had been on the orbital platform a few months ago, and it hadn't been able to access Rae's programming until after they activated a version of her onboard.

"So what now? Do we cut down the tree? Set it on fire? What?" he asked.

"None of those things. Not unless you want to take the plat's entire system offline. I need to repair the damage it did and strip out all the infected code. When I do that, the ghost will react."

"To protect itself and the damage it's already wrought," Ruin said.

"Yup. And once I scrub this system, I'll know how to delete it, too."

He took up a position behind her, summoning the kes'tarv with a thought. "Do what you need to. I'll make sure our ghost doesn't interfere."

He felt a brief touch on his shoulder as she said, "Be back soon."

Then she went silent, and he knew she was entirely consumed by her task. This was why he'd insisted on accompanying her, and why Wreckage was guarding her physical body. When a cyber-jockey was fully jacked, they were completely unaware of what was happening to their body. Now Jade was doing something similar yet again, extending most of her awareness and focus into the system she was infiltrating. She needed him to stand guard and protect her from anything that might try to attack them in this strange place.

The silence soothed him in the same way the forest did, but he didn't allow himself to relax. He needed to stay alert and scan for a threat he might not recognize if he wasn't paying attention.

Time moved differently in this place, making it feel like Jade had been gone for a long time. A quick check of his onboard system informed him it had only been four minutes and nineteen seconds.

He chuckled ruefully at himself and rolled his shoulders automatically to ease some of his tension. Then he remembered he didn't have a body and the tension he felt was all in his mind. It made the entire experience even more surreal. Here he was, floating in a forest that wasn't a forest, on guard against a threat that might look like anything or nothing at all.

He twirled his kes'tarv idly and settled in to wait.

At nine minutes and forty-two seconds, he saw it—the thing that didn't belong. His mind told him it was a *kopaki*, a creature native to this planet, but that wasn't possible. They weren't even on Liberty right now, and what he could see wasn't *right*. It was almost invisible for one thing, the shadowy form more translucent than the more solid avatars he and Jade had. It was also bigger than any *kopaki* he'd ever seen, with impossibly long claws and fangs the length of his index finger. At least, that's what he thought he saw, but he only got a glimpse before it disappeared.

This was the program they'd come here to kill. It had to be. Jade had told him his mind would recognize the threat, and it had. That's why he perceived it to be one of the most dangerous predators on the planet.

"Jade, I don't know if you can hear me, but we have company. Whatever you're doing, our ghost doesn't like it. Keep going."

He spotted a flicker of movement to his right and spun in that direction, but the thing was already gone. Then it appeared above and to the left, forcing him to move again so he was between this thing and Jade.

It lingered for a few seconds before vanishing again. Ruin returned to his former position, his instincts telling him the thing was trying to draw him out, so he'd leave Jade open to attack. This thing wasn't after him. He was just in its way. Jade was its real target.

"You can't have her," Ruin said to the empty air, not caring if the thing could understand him or not.

It appeared again, rushing at him from below. He aimed the lower tip of the weapon at the digital ghost and fired, not even sure what that would do in this place.

A blast of brilliant white light erupted from the end of the staff. It struck the oncoming thing in the chest, and it immediately disappeared. *Fraxx.* Had that done anything to wound this thing? He had no idea, but something told him he'd need more than one weapon to keep this thing away from Jade.

Then Jade's words came back to him. *"You are a weapon. Reality is what we make of it."*

Holding that thought in his mind, he envisioned a shield tall and wide enough to keep the thing at bay. All he had to do was buy Jade enough time to finish the job. If he killed it before she did, all the better.

The next attack came from above. The ghost learned quickly, and this time it managed to camouflage itself until it was almost on top of them. Ruin raised the shield over his head just in time. The thing uttered a vicious hiss of crackling static as it struck the shield and bounced away.

He scanned the area, his senses on high alert.

"I'm almost done. You said we had company. Is it still here?" Jade asked, her voice startling him.

"It's here, pissed off, and doing its best to kill you. I'm not sure my weapons are doing much damage. It's hard to tell since I can barely see this thing."

"That explains it. I'm trying to unravel its matrix right now and it's easier than it should be. Whatever you're doing, keep it up. You're making my job easier."

"Will do. Let's kill this thing and go home."

He hovered in midair, looking everywhere for any sign of the ghost. Nothing.

Seconds ticked by, his nonexistent skin prickling with anticipation as he waited for the thing to show itself. Still nothing.

Then he heard it. The same static-filled hissing noise as before. And it was coming from behind him.

Ruin spun, coming face to face with the thing as it flew past the tree and Jade. This time, *he* was its target. It was too close for the shield to work, so he instinctively dropped it. In this place, that meant the construct came apart and was reabsorbed into his body, but he was too busy to watch it happen.

He raised his staff and jammed it between the ghost's jaws. It slavered and gnawed on the shaft, but it stayed intact. That gave Ruin leverage and the ability to keep the thing's head away from him.

He expected it to tear into him with its claws, but that's not what happened. Instead, it started to glow with a sickly greenish-black light that made it possible to see clearly. A high-pitched electronic shriek rose from the thing, the light and noise intensifying with every passing second.

He grappled with the thing, desperately fighting to move it away from Jade. He managed to kick his lower half free and then raised both legs to his chest and drove his feet against its muzzle as he released the kes'tarv. He flew away from the thing, which was now little more than an orb of pulsating light and sound.

He threw up another shield, this one even larger than the last.

"I got it!" Jade announced. He snapped his head around to look her way.

Her mouth was turned up in a triumphant grin,

but her eyes were wide with fear as she took in the scene.

"Ruin. No!" She rushed at him, her arms reaching, her expression frantic.

Then, the thing behind him exploded, and all the light faded away. The last thing he saw was Jade's beautiful face... and then there was nothing but darkness.

18

———

WRECKAGE HAD NEVER SPENT much time in a med-center until coming to Haven, but lately he couldn't get away from the place. It was even stranger to be here for Ruin. His batch-brother had gone and done the same stupid thing Wreckage had so many years ago. He'd put himself in harm's way to protect someone else. The *fraxxing* idiot was lucky to be alive. Cyborgs were hardened against EMPs, but that didn't help much if you were standing at ground zero when it went off.

He sat beside Ruin's bed, waiting for the fool to wake up. Guilt gnawed at him every minute. He'd gone into cyberspace before. Ruin hadn't. Would things have gone differently if they'd changed places?

Jade was nestled in his lap, her head on his shoulder and her eyes closed. The doctor had ordered her to rest, but Wreckage knew she was still awake.

She wouldn't sleep until Ruin came back to them. Neither would he.

"You're doing it again," Jade said without lifting her head.

"Doing what?" he had no idea what she was talking about.

"Blaming yourself. You think you should have been the one to go in with me. Don't you?"

"How could you possibly know that?"

"Because I know you. The two of you have the same bad habit of taking responsibility for everything, even when you have no reason to feel guilty. If the roles were reversed, Ruin would be sitting in this chair right now, feeling exactly the same way."

She was right, dammit. "Maybe."

"No maybe about it. And neither of you is to blame for what happened. The Shadows inserted a semi-sentient AI into our systems."

"Tell me again what exactly this thing was supposed to do?" She'd given him a general explanation of what she'd found, but they hadn't had time to talk until now.

"Basically? It was a digital spy. It snooped through anything that wasn't encrypted, looking for useful information. It stored it in a partitioned section of the plat's system, which someone accessed from time to time. My best guess is that the agent for the Grays, or the Shadows, whatever we're calling them now, must have done it. Yardan and Skye will need to investigate before we can be sure."

"But spying wasn't all it was supposed to do. Otherwise, it wouldn't have attacked you."

"I was too busy destroying the code to get a good look at it, but from what I saw, I think it had a self-defense subroutine. Those are fairly common in spyware. They're just supposed to stop the program from being discovered."

Wreckage scowled. Even though he had hardware and software imbedded in his body, he didn't have much of an idea how any of it worked. "This one went a lot further than simply avoiding detection. Why?"

Jade raised her head. "Because someone designed that thing without including the standard protocols that forbid any artificial lifeform from harming an organic being. I've heard rumors about other AIs like this, but I've never seen one. Supposedly, the Gray Men had one at one point, but that's just conjecture. No one knows if it's true or not."

"If they had one at some point, it makes sense they'd build another." The thought didn't sit well with him. How did they fight a digital enemy? They didn't have Jade's abilities in cyberspace. No one did except for Phaedra, and she wouldn't be online again until after her baby was born.

"We're watching now, though. The rest of the team is already reviewing all our protocols. We'll figure out where the holes are and plug them. If the Shadows or anyone else try to slip another spy into our network, we'll be ready and waiting for them." Jade raised her head and looked at Ruin. "I think we need to recruit more cyborgs, though. You all seem to have a natural affinity for it. If even just a few agreed to have the implants, we'd be in a far better position."

"You want recruits?" Wreckage grinned. "We should start by asking the kids."

"The kids?" She turned to look at him. "Do you think that's really the best way to address them?"

He shrugged. "It's how I've always thought of them. I've just never said it out loud until now."

"Kids," she spoke the word like she was testing it. "I like it. This means I've got kids now, but they're all adults with their own lives, so I won't worry about screwing up as a parent."

"Well, if you want to claim them as your kids, you'll have to move in with us."

She laughed. "Don't tell me you told Thrash the truth just so you could use that argument."

"I admit to nothing."

He hadn't intended to say anything to the others. Not until Ruin was awake and they could do it together. But fate had other plans.

Striker had tried to contact Ruin and received an offline notice. They all knew what that meant—either Ruin was unconscious or dead. He'd immediately messaged Wreckage to find out what was going on, and before he knew it, word had spread. Almost every cyborg in the colony was lurking in the waiting room or outside the med-center, waiting for news.

Thrash hadn't been content to wait with the others. He'd ignored the doctor and walked into Ruin's room.

"If he dies before someone tells me the truth, I'm going to be pissed."

"He's not going to die," Jade had said.

Thrash had relaxed a little. "Good. But I still want to know why we look so much alike."

Wreckage was too tired to lie any longer, so he'd told Thrash the truth. All of it. Then he'd waited for the reaction. It wasn't what he expected. Thrash leaned against the nearest wall and grinned. "Holy *fraxx*. We're family?"

"We are," he'd confirmed.

Jade had left her chair and crossed the room to give Thrash a hug. "Welcome to the family. Now, will you finally stop flirting with me?"

"Uh, yeah. Definitely." The big cyborg had actually blushed at that. Then he'd come over to grip Wreckage's shoulder. "Family. I thought I'd lost all of mine." Then his grip tightened. "Later, we're going to have a talk about why you've kept this a secret for so long."

"Later," Wreckage had agreed.

And that was it. No anger. No venom. No guilt. At least, not yet. When Ruin woke up and learned their secret was out, he'd be madder than a Torski with a toothache, but they'd deal with that when it happened.

"I still can't believe you spilled the beans before Ruin woke up. He's going to be pissed at you," Jade said, but her tone was light, and she was smiling a little.

"I'll tell him to run around the cabin until he feels better. It seems to work for him."

Jade shook her head, her lips twitching into a grin that quickly faded as she lifted Ruin's limp hand from her lap. "How much longer do you think he'll be out? I thought the doctor said he'd be awake by now."

"She said he'd be awake soon, sweetling. She didn't give us an exact time. All his systems were disrupted by that EMP the ghost emitted as it died. It will take time for his onboard network to do a system check and reboot."

"Do you think he knows we're here?" she asked.

"Definitely. I've been through this. Though I was running away from the source instead of standing on top of it. You know that feeling when you're almost awake but you're still caught up in a dream? Things come in flashes, and you can't tell what's part of the dream and what's real? That's what it's like. He'll be groggy and grumpy, but that's all."

Ruin groaned and opened his eyes. "For the last time, I am not grumpy!"

Jade gave a squeal of joy and gripped Ruin's hand in both of hers. "Yeah, you are. But I love you anyway. Welcome back. And don't ever do that again!"

"Do what?" Ruin looked around him, confused. "What happened and where am I?"

"The ghost hit you with an EMP as it died. Now, you're in the med-center." Wreckage grinned at him. "Threw yourself into harm's way to protect someone else. Who's the *fraxxing* idiot now?"

"It's still you. EMPs aren't usually fatal. Bounder mines are."

"Point to you," Wreckage admitted. "Glad you're back with us. How are you feeling?" As he spoke, he sent a message to Thrash and the others, letting them know Ruin was awake.

"Groggy but not grumpy." Ruin looked at Jade. "You killed it? And you're okay. You must be, or Wreck wouldn't let you be on your feet."

"*We* killed it." She stressed the first word. "You weakened it and kept it off of me long enough for me to destroy its matrix."

Ruin nodded and relaxed into his pillow. "Good. Anything else I need to know about?"

"Not much." Thrash breezed into the room with Dr. Clark right behind him, looking annoyed. "I do have one question for you, though." He grinned. "Can I call you Dad?"

"What? No! Wreck, what the *fraxx* did you tell him? I'm out for a few hours and you do this? That's minus several million points for you."

"It wasn't planned," Wreckage said with a shrug. "It just kind of came up."

Jade snickered. "Yeah, because Thrash is more like the two of you than I realized. He doesn't just look like you. He's got your stubborn attitude, too."

"Jade, you let this happen?" Ruin demanded.

"Relax, Ru. It was time for the truth to come out. And no one's angry about it," she said and patted his hand.

"Yeah. Seems we were wrong about that," Wreckage said. He couldn't stop smiling. Somehow, they'd made it through everything and were still together.

Jade grinned. "I guess that means that point goes to me."

Ruin's jaw relaxed and his brow smoothed. "You're playing the game now?"

Jade nodded.

"And what are you going to want as a reward when you get to ten points?" Wreckage asked.

She flashed them both a wicked grin. "Orgasms of course."

Thrash barked out a laugh and clapped his hands over his ears. "That's it. I've heard enough. This was more fun before I knew the two of you were my parents. Now it's just weird."

He fled the room. Dr. Clark came over to join them. "Do I want to know what that's about?"

"Probably not," Wreckage said.

Jade laughed and took his hand in hers. "I think

Thrash just discovered the downside to uncovering a secret."

"Serves him right," Ruin muttered.

"But we're done with secrets now." Jade beamed at them both, the warmth of her smile making him melt inside. "Aren't we?"

Wreckage wrapped her in his arms and kissed her. "No more secrets. Just you, us, and a lifetime of laughter."

She kissed him back, still holding Ruin's hand. "*And orgasms,*" she sent to them both via her new link. "*Can't forget about those.*"

EPILOGUE

THE LATE SPRING sunshine was glorious. Jade had enjoyed the winter snows and the blush of early spring, but this was her new favorite season. Everything was fresh and new, from the grass beneath her feet to the blossoms blooming all around her.

Their cabin was undergoing a transformation, too. The clearing buzzed with activity as beings worked tirelessly to create their new home. Jade moved among them, handing out drinks and snacks to anyone who wanted them, all while supervising the changes taking place.

The cabin Wreckage and Ruin had built themselves now formed the center of a larger structure, one built with help from their friends and newly claimed family. Everyone knew the location now, and visitors were common, though they were smart enough not to arrive unannounced.

A new, far larger kitchen was almost complete. It had all the appliances of a modern home, powered by a piece of Vardarian tech that would keep the entire home running for decades.

Ruin passed by with several freshly planed planks over his shoulder. "Drink?" She offered him a glass. "Nope. But I do need a kiss."

He caught her around the waist and pulled her in against his bare chest, his mouth swooping down to claim hers. He smelled of sweat and sawdust, but he tasted like perfection as his tongue danced with hers for a brief moment before he raised his head and grinned. "You're in demand today, sweetling."

"Damn right she is." Ruin's voice was a low rumble that made her pulse skitter. She turned and found herself pulled into another bare-chested embrace. Ruin kissed her hard, his fingers running up the back of her neck to tangle in her hair.

"Oh *fraxx*, they're at it again! Oi, you three. Get a room. Us kids don't need to see that sort of thing," Thrash called out from across the clearing.

"Blood or not, I'm going to kill him someday," Ruin said, his lips still on hers.

"No, you won't. We just need to find him a nice woman to distract him." Jade had been keeping an eye on the newest arrivals, but so far none of them were ready to join the colony, and she didn't get the sense any of them were the right fit for Thrash. She'd keep looking, though. After all, if she could find the loves of her life in Haven, why couldn't everyone else?

Standing in the clearing surrounded by family, friends, and the two men who had claimed her heart, Jade could believe that anything was possible. She'd come to this place as a prisoner, broken and abused. Now she had everything she'd ever wanted, and more than she'd dared to hope for.

"I love you both so much," she whispered, knowing they would hear her.

"And we love you, little goddess. Always and forever." Ruin kissed her softly as Wreckage dropped a kiss to the top of her hair.

"Always and forever," she repeated, meaning every word. It was a promise they made to each other every day and would for the rest of their lives.

Thank You for Reading Her Cyborg Rangers

I hope you enjoyed Jade, Wreckage, and Ruin's story. Would you like to read a special bonus epilogue to this story? Sign up for my newsletter here: subscribepage.io/Bonuscontent

If you're looking for more Sci-fi romances like this one, I invite you to explore the other books in the Drift universe, which now Include Haven Colony, Nova Force and the original Drift series.

ABOUT THE AUTHOR

Susan lives out on the Canadian west coast surrounded by open water, dear family, and good friends. She's jumped out of perfectly good airplanes on purpose and accidentally swum with sharks on the Great Barrier Reef.

If the world ends, she plans to survive as the spunky, comedic sidekick to the heroes of the new world, because she's too damned short and out of shape to make it on her own for long.

You can find out more about Susan and her books at:
www.susanhayes.ca

www.ingramcontent.com/pod-product-compliance
Lightning Source LLC
Chambersburg PA
CBHW061241310726
48971CB00007B/2161